# FRACTURED AND OTHER FAIRY TALES

# FRACTURED AND OTHER FAIRY TALES

William Thompson

ISBN: 1518835996
ISBN 13: 9781518835995
Library of Congress Control Number: 2015918053
CreateSpace Independent Publishing Platform
North Charleston, South Carolina

*For my daughters*
*In memory of many stories*

## Acknowledgments

Most of these stories were originally published on my blog, Of Other Worlds: A Children's Literature Blog. I wish to thank everyone who read and commented on the stories, and who had as much joy reading them as I had in writing them.

# Contents

## Red Riding Hood, or Why You Should Listen to Your Granny

R ed stepped briskly along the path. It was early, and she thought she could get to Granny's by late morning. Granny hadn't been feeling so well this past week, and Red was bringing her a few things to lift her spirits.

The forest was deep and dark, but Red knew she would be fine as long as she stuck to the path. That was the first rule of traveling through the forest—stick to the path. The second rule was not talking to strangers, especially large, hairy strangers who pretended to be kind and helpful. But in case she did meet such a stranger, Red had just what she needed in the pocket of her cloak.

Red came to a giant oak in the path. It was a tricky spot because she couldn't see ahead or behind as she came around the tree. The path went down into a little dell, and it came up and around the far side of the oak.

Red reached inside her cloak and pulled out her phone. If she was going to have company, then she would have it here. Sure enough, Red saw a tall, slouching figure come onto the path just ahead.

Red stepped quickly back behind the giant oak. She thumbed her phone.

"Hello, Red," came Granny's voice. "Are you on your way?"

"Yes," said Red in a half whisper. "But I have company on the path."

"You know what to do, dear," said Granny. "I'll see you soon, and we can have tea."

Red pocketed her phone and once again stepped out onto the path. Reaching again under her cloak, she took the can of bear spray in hand. This stranger was about to get a surprise.

Looking wide-eyed and innocent, Red walked along the path toward the wolf that waited. He tried to smile ingratiatingly. Red almost felt sorry for the big brute.

"Good morning, little girl," said the wolf. "And where are you off to this fine morning?" He was working his jaws hard to hide his slavering chops.

"Good morning," said Red. "I'm just off to visit my Granny." And with that, she pulled the bear spray from beneath her cloak and let him have it full in the face.

Well, that wolf howled and yowled, and he stumbled back off the path. Red repocketed her spray and carried on, and for a long time she heard the wolf yammering and crashing through the forest.

That's the end of that, thought Red, smugly. But little girls are not as wise as old grannies in the ways of wily wolves.

The wolf found a pool in the forest and ducked his head repeatedly until the sting lessened in his eyes and nose. "The little wretch," he said to himself, grimly. "I'll have that little brat—and her granny as well." And with that the wolf loped through the forest in search of Granny's house.

By that time, Red had reached Granny's, and she was busily unpacking her basket and telling Granny all about her adventure in the forest. But Granny was less impressed than Red expected. Remember, grannies are wiser in the ways of wolves and other unpleasantness in the forest than little girls.

Granny patted Red's cheek. "Very good, dear," she said. "But we have more to do."

Granny had Red help her with a large cauldron that they maneuvered onto the fire. They filled it with water and stoked the fire. Soon the water in the cauldron was roiling and boiling, and Granny's face took on an expectant expression. They didn't have to wait long.

A knock came at the door. Red looked with alarm at her Granny, but the old woman simply sat by the fire.

"Oh, please, old granny," said a plaintive voice from outside the door. "Open up and let in a poor, starving stranger."

Granny rolled her eyes. "Always the same trick," she muttered.

The wolf, for it was indeed the wolf outside the door, stared in disgust at the little house. He knew the old lady was too cunning to just open the door. He thought of huffing and puffing, but that one didn't always work. Eyeing a tree beside the house, he thought of a better plan. He scrambled up the tree, and with a swing and a grunt, he stood next to the chimney.

He didn't like the look of the smoke coming from the chimney, but he was bent on revenge and a meal, so in headfirst he went.

Red was still standing, watching Granny by the fire. She heard the wolf on the roof, and feeling suddenly afraid, she heard him scrambling down the chimney.

Now, if you know anything about chimneys, you will know they are full of smoke and soot.

That gave Granny her edge. When the wolf popped his head out of the chimney, he shook his head and gave a terrific sneeze. Quick as a flash, Granny reached out and gave his ears a terrific tug. The wolf fell straight into the pot of roiling, boiling water. And that was the end of him.

When the local woodsman, swinging his great, sharp axe, came striding through the forest, he knocked at Granny's door. There he found Granny and Red having tea and cake at the table. He was a little disappointed not to have a shot at the wolf, but he was very glad to join them for tea.

## Goldilocks and the Three Pigs

Once there was a little girl who lived with her mother at the edge of the forest. Her name was Goldilocks, for she had a great mane of golden curls.

One day, the mother said to Goldilocks, "I want you to take this basket to your grandma. She's not feeling well, and a pot of broth and some fresh biscuits and jam will do her good."

"Very well, Mother," said Goldilocks, and she grabbed up her cloak.

"Now, listen to me," said her mother, sternly. "You go straight to Grandma's. Don't dawdle, and don't leave the path." The mother had to be stern, for she knew that Goldilocks was a bit of an airhead, as much as she hated to admit such a thing about her own daughter.

Grandma lived on the other side of a danger-ous wood, and Goldilocks had the attention span of a gnat.

"I'll stay on the path, Mother. Don't wor-ry." And Goldilocks caught up the basket and skipped off through the garden to the edge of the wood.

To her credit, Goldilocks stayed on the forest path—for at least ten minutes. But there were so many interesting things to see. She passed a lovely little brook, splashing and chattering to itself, and she saw a patch of buttercups that made her gasp in delight. Soon enough, she had wandered from the path and was lost in the wood.

But Goldilocks was unperturbed. She skipped along through the trees until she came to a clearing, and right in the center was a little house built of straw.

"How cute," said Goldilocks to herself, and she skipped up to the door and peered inside.

No one was home. The house had a little bed and a little table and chair. On the table was a little bowl, and it was full of something, just waiting for the owner to come home. On the wall, just above the table, was a picture of a smiling, mother pig.

Goldilocks was hungry from her walk through the wood. "I don't suppose," she said to herself, "it would matter if I had just a taste?"

She caught up a spoon, scooped out some of the stew, and put the whole spoonful into her mouth. And what a surprise she got. It was terrible.

Turnip stew, thought Goldilocks. Ick! Yuck! Gag!

And she rushed out of the house and spat out the stew. "That has to be the vilest thing I've ever tasted," she said, once her mouth was empty. She thought of the fresh biscuits and jam in her basket, but those were for Grandma. And off Goldilocks skipped.

On and on through the forest she went, until she came to another clearing. And in the center was a little house made of sticks. This time, Goldilocks approached with a little more caution. She peeped inside the door, and she saw another little bed and little table set with a bowl of stew. On the wall was a picture of the same smiling, mother pig.

Stepping inside and up to the table, Goldilocks leaned down and took a sniff, prodding the stuff with the spoon.

Ugh! Turnip stew, again! The smell was enough to make her gag. And she turned and ran out of the house.

On and on she went, until she came to another clearing and another little house. This one was made of brick, and it had frilly curtains at the windows.

"How sweet!" exclaimed Goldilocks. She went inside, and this time she found a freshly baked apple pie and a jug of thick cream on the table.

"Excellent," said Goldilocks, and she sat down, poured cream onto the pie, and began to eat. She ate and ate, for her walk had made her very hungry.

She didn't stop until the plate was clean. But a walk through the forest and an entire pie can have an effect. Goldilocks suddenly felt sleepy, and then she felt a little sick.

"Oh dear," she said. "I think I need to lie down."

Goldilocks looked about. She found a tiny room, and inside was a neat little bed. Goldilocks curled up on the bed, and with a little moan, she was soon fast asleep.

About the same time as Goldilocks was finishing the pie, the three pigs were making their way home from the market. They were sharp eyed and sharp eared, for they knew the wolf was lurking in the neighborhood and was quite ready to help himself to pig, if he could get it.

They went along until they came to the house of the first pig—the house made of straw. "Someone's been in here," said the first pig to his brothers. The three of them peeped inside and saw the spoon sticking out of the bowl of turnip stew.

"It's the wolf!" they cried. And as a bunch, they tore through the woods until they came to the house of the second pig—the house of sticks.

As they came inside and shut the door, they turned and suddenly saw the spoon sticking out of the bowl of stew. "The wolf!" they cried, and they left the house in a panic.

"We'll be safe at my house," said the third pig, puffing along behind his brothers.

They came to the house of brick, got inside, and shut the door. "Thank goodness," they said to one another.

But just then, they heard a sound coming from the little bedroom. It was a snuffling, grunting snore, followed by a sigh. Then they saw the empty pie plate and empty jug on the table. "The wolf!" they cried. And the three pigs tore out of the house and ran and ran and ran until they came back to their mother's house, where they told her all about their adventures in the forest. Much to their mother's chagrin, they swore they would never leave her again.

As for Goldilocks, she had a refreshing nap. When she woke, she gathered up her basket and continued on her way. As luck would have it, she found the forest path, and this time she followed it right to her grandma's house.

"Have a nice walk, dear?" said the grandma to Goldilocks.

"Oh, Grandma!" cried Goldilocks. "I've had so many adventures."

And just as wise grandmas do, she sat Goldilocks down, gave her some tea and a sandwich, and listened to the tale of her adventures in the forest.

They had a lovely visit, and when the afternoon got late, the grandma took a great cudgel from behind the door, which she kept there in case of unwelcome visitors, and together, they set off through the forest for home.

## POSTSCRIPT

The wolf was indeed on the prowl that day. He was hungry for a fat little porker. He came to the house of straw. "Little pig, little pig!" he cried. "Open up, or I'll huff, and I'll puff, and I'll blow in your door!"

But to his surprise, he saw the door was open, and no one was home.

Great, he thought. He rushed through the woods until he came to the house of sticks.

"Little pig, little pig!" he cried. "Open up, or I'll huff, and I'll puff, and I'll blow in your door!"

No answer.

The wolf nudged open the door, and he saw that this house was empty as well. Those little pigs are trying to make a fool of me, he thought, angrier than ever.

He ran and he ran until he came to the house of brick. "Little pig, little pig!" he cried. "Open up, or I'll huff, and I'll puff, and I'll blow in your door!"

Nothing.

"What's wrong with the world?" said the wolf to himself. He pushed open the door. He saw the empty pie plate, the empty jug, and a long, golden hair that lay curled on the floor.

"Nuts!" said the wolf. And he left. He was so disgusted that, after that day, he became a vegetarian. Eventually, he opened a restaurant at the edge of the forest and called it the Veggie Platter. Animals came from miles around to visit the place, and they said that nowhere could you get a better vegetarian stew.

## POST-POSTSCRIPT

The three bears got up the morning Goldilocks was to make her way to her grandma's house.

Mama Bear made porridge, but it was too hot to eat. She set the porridge on the table to cool, and then she, Papa Bear, and Baby Bear went into the forest to gather berries. When they came home, each lugging a bucket of berries, they found their porridge ready to eat. They had a lovely breakfast and a quiet day, and they never did meet Goldilocks.

## Hansel and Gretel, or The Way to Start Your Own Franchise

"Y ou're a dweeb," said Gretel to her brother, who was at that moment trying to catch a butterfly that was pertched on a branch.

"But I just want to catch it so I can draw it," said Hansel. "I'll let it go again."

Gretel shook her head. She and her brother lived with their father and stepmother at the edge of a great forest. Hansel was a short, round boy who loved to wander in the forest, but Gretel was tall and lanky, and she was interested in ways to make money, as the family was very poor. The father was a woodcutter. You would think that in a time when most people heated their little homes with wood fires that he would do all right. But he didn't. He piled the wood he gathered from the forest in untidy heaps, and when people came shopping for wood, they saw the mess and politely said they were just browsing.

Gretel was frustrated with her father. "Presentation is everything. Don't you get it?"

But her father didn't understand. He simply looked bewildered, and he went into the forest to cut more wood.

"We have to do something," said Gretel to her brother one evening. "We need a marketing plan. Father is never going to sell any wood this way."

"Hush," said Hansel. "What are they saying in the other room?"

The children listened, and much to their horror, they heard their stepmother plotting to get rid of them.

"Children are so expensive to raise," said the stepmother. "Soon they'll be teenagers, and then there will be no end to the costs. Have you thought about all the stuff they'll want? Have you thought about university expenses?"

Their father said nothing.

"Tomorrow," said the stepmother, "I want you to take the children into the forest and leave them there. That way, we can have our own lives and not worry about having to pay for two lazy children."

"Lazy," muttered Gretel. "Look who's talking."

But now that Gretel knew of her stepmother's plot, she had a plan of her own. "Tomorrow, before dawn," she whispered to Hansel, "we get out of here."

"All right," said Hansel, but he couldn't help a tear from rolling down his plump cheek at the hardness of the world.

The next morning, while their father and stepmother were still sleeping, Hansel and Gretel slipped out of the house. As Hansel was the one who knew his way about the forest, he led the way.

"Be sure to cover our tracks," said Gretel as they walked along.

"Don't worry," said Hansel. "They'll never find us."

When their father got up that morning, he found that his children had run away, carrying their few possessions with them. In spite of his wife's exclamations of joy at the disappearance of the children, their father searched through the forest, hunting high and low. But he never found them, and he assumed his children had been eaten by wild animals. He went home and sat by the fire, for he was sad, and in spite of all her nagging, the husband refused to cut anymore wood.

As for the children, they wandered through the wood, never seeming to get anywhere.

They stopped once to eat the bread that Gretel had stolen from the pantry, but by the time the moon was shining high overhead, the children were so tired that they just lay down beneath a tree to sleep.

"We're lost," said Gretel to her brother as she stared up at the moon. "Nice going, genius."

"Don't worry," said Hansel. "Who knows what tomorrow will bring."

And the children fell fast asleep in the forest.

The next morning, the children got up and wandered on through the trees. Soon, they came to an open space, and standing in the middle of the little meadow was a tiny house made of gingerbread. The posts that held up the porch roof were made of sugar candy, and icing dotted with gumdrops coated every surface.

"That doesn't look suspicious at all," said Gretel.

But Hansel had already run forward and was scooping icing and gumdrops into his mouth. "Tastes good!" he cried, breaking off a bit of gingerbread from a windowsill.

Just then, the door opened, and out hobbled an old witch. Of course she was a witch, and she caught Hansel by the neck and stuffed him into a sack she carried in her other hand.

"A tasty, tasty treat," said the old witch in a voice that crackled like a fire. "Now, just you come here," she said to Gretel, "and you can join your brother."

But Gretel wasn't as stupid as all that. "Please don't eat my brother!" cried Gretel in her best afraid-little-girl voice. "If you agree not to eat my brother, I'll work for you. I'll do all of your chores and keep this place spick and span."

The witch peered at Gretel out of red eyes. "Perhaps," she murmured. "How about you come inside and show me what you can do?" The old witch was really planning to get Gretel into the house so she could cook her, but she was too used to easy prey, and she didn't know what she was getting herself in for.

Gretel came into the house and looked around. She saw the possibilities at once. It was a snug little place, and out back there was a wide patio, where the witch kept cages for her victims.

The old witch had thrown Hansel into a cage, sack and all, and locked the door, chuckling and smacking her old lips.

Hansel poked his head out of the sack and stared wildly around. "You just let me out of this cage!" he shouted at the witch.

"You keep your shirt on," said the witch to Hansel. "Your sister says she'll work for me, and if she's a good girl, then maybe I won't eat you."

She turned to Gretel. "I have this pan of brownies ready for baking. You just put your head inside the oven and see if it's hot enough."

Gretel rolled her eyes. Was the old woman kidding?

But in her sweetest little-girl voice, Gretel said, "I've never done that before. Can you show me once so I understand what you mean?"

"Stupid child!" cried the witch. "Like this." And she yanked open the oven door and stuck her head inside.

Quick as a flash, Gretel caught the old witch by the neck. "Now listen here, you old hag," said Gretel, through clenched teeth. "Your baking days are done. There are going to be a few changes around here."

And there were. Gretel let Hansel out of his cage, and she stuffed in the witch. She kept the old woman locked up until she agreed not to trap and eat kids anymore.

Gretel swept and cleaned that little cottage. She found heaps of gold in the corners, and she used it to buy a new oven and a barista machine. She ordered tables and chairs for the patio, and she got rid of the cages. When she was ready, she had signs pointing the way to the cottage. They read: Treats by "Gretel." And in no time, she was open for business.

The old witch worked as a server, while Gretel baked, made candy, and ran the barista machine. People came from miles around to sit on the patio, sip coffee, and sample Gretel's treats. Even her stepmother and father eventually found their way to the shop. Gretel didn't feel much like forgiving them, so she hired them as her cleaning staff and put them to work.

And as for Hansel, he wasn't interested in Gretel's business, but he came regularly to visit. He didn't like the manic gleam that Gretel got in her eye as she ordered around her staff and counted up her profits. But he decided not to worry about it. He mostly liked to wander the forest, getting to know the trees and the habits of the animals. And really, after a day of wandering in the forest, there was nothing like coming back to Gretel's shop for a quiet coffee and a slice of her key lime pie.

# The Frog Prince, or
# A Girl's Best Friend

Once upon a time, there was a widow who lived with her daughter at the edge of a village. The widow baked bread for people in the village, and she had to work hard. Every day, she tried to get her daughter to help, but Molly, for that was her name, was always running off to play.

"If only," cried the widow, "I had a daughter who was of some use in the kitchen!"

But Molly wasn't any use in the kitchen or out of it. She would take her prized possession, a small golden ball, and she would run out to the forest to play.

One day, Molly came upon a pool in the forest. It was deep and clear, surrounded by rocks and ferns, and she bent over to have a look. And with a plop, her golden ball disappeared into the pool.

"Woe is me!" cried Molly. "What will I do? I've lost my golden ball in the pool!" And she sat down and began to cry.

"What's troubling you, little maid?" asked a voice.

Molly stopped blubbering long enough to look up, and there, sitting at the edge of the pool, was a hideous old frog.

Molly didn't mind frogs, and she blinked away her tears and stared at him curiously. "I've never met a talking frog before," she said.

"I'm actually a prince under an enchantment," said the frog impressively. "If you promise to take me home, let me eat from your little plate, and let me sleep in your little bed, I will fetch your golden ball from the depths of this pool."

"A prince," said Molly, a little doubtfully. She had only ever heard of such things in fairy tales. And sleep in her bed? She wasn't sure if her mother would want that.

She stared hard at the frog. "If you fetch my golden ball, then I promise to take you home. We'll see about the sleeping arrangements."

"Fair enough," gulped the frog. And with a kick and a splash, he dove into the pool.

He was a long time under the water, so long that Molly began to wonder if he was ever going to come back. And then, with a splash and a splat, the frog was sitting on one of the stones. Giving a great croak, he spat the golden ball into Molly's lap. And she was so delighted, she sprang up and ran all the way home, forgetting her promise to the frog. She might have remembered, but as soon as she came in the door, her mother put her to work.

"Fill the wood box, you lazy thing," she scolded. "And when you are done with that, you can set the table for dinner."

Molly set to work, and in no time at all, she had the wood box filled, and she and her mother were sitting at the table eating soup and breaking off chunks of steaming, crackling bread.

Just then, there came a knock at the door. "Young maid," cried a voice. "Keep your promise. Let me sit at the table and eat from your plate."

Molly ran to the door, and there was the frog, bobbing and puffing.

"What is that slimy thing?" asked her mother, peering over Molly's shoulder.

"It's a prince under an enchantment," said Molly. "I promised that I would let him eat from my plate if he got my golden ball from the pool."

"Well," said the widow, "a promise is a promise. Bring the silly thing into the house, but keep it out of my way."

Molly let the frog eat from her plate, but when it came time for bed, she found a box, and she stuffed the frog inside.

"Young maid," cried the frog, plaintively. "You promised to let me sleep in your bed, so keep your promise."

"You are a slimy frog, wet and icky," said Molly. "You can sleep in the box."

After that, the frog would sit at the table and eat from Molly's plate, but at night she stuffed him back in his box. He complained and complained.

"You promised," he would say. "You promised to let me sleep in your bed. I found your golden ball, and you must keep your promise."

"Do you ever shut up?" cried Molly. And she got so tired of hearing him complain, she covered the box with a quilt to muffle his voice. After a week, she'd had enough. She took the frog in his box into the forest where she found the pool.

"Back you go," she said, "enchanted prince, or no."

Upending the box, she dumped the frog into the water. Just as she did, a great fish came up from the depths and swallowed the frog with a snap.

"Oh," cried Molly. "That wasn't very nice." And she grabbed the fish and heaved him out of the pool.

The fish landed on the ground with a great splat. "Young maiden, young maiden," cried the fish. "If you put me back into the water, I will grant you three wishes."

"Three wishes," said Molly doubtfully. "Are you something enchanted as well?"

"Yes, yes!" cried the fish. "I will grant you three wishes, any wishes you like, as long as you put me back in the pool."

But listening to enchanted creatures had gotten Molly into trouble from the start. "Cough up the frog, and then we can talk," said Molly.

With a great, belching heave, the fish coughed up the frog. For his part, the frog was a little worse for wear, having been in the stomach of the fish, and he just lay there on the ground, looking pathetic and half dead.

"Now," said Molly, "you owe me some wishes."

"Fair enough," gasped the fish. "But make it quick. I have to get back into the pool."

"First," said Molly, "if that frog is a prince, then change him back. And second, give my mother enough money so she doesn't have to work so hard. And finally, I want a pet, and I don't want it to be a frog. Perhaps a nice dog?"

Maybe the fish didn't entirely understand. He was lying there gasping out his life, so he might not have heard correctly. At any rate, he took a shortcut. With a popping flash, the frog disappeared, but in its place, there wasn't a prince, but a great, droopy-eared red setter. He panted once and gave a whine, and Molly was delighted. She picked up the fish and dropped him back into the pool.

Molly went home with her new pet, and she found that her mother had suddenly come into some money, enough to open a bakery and hire some help. The widow became the most famous baker in the kingdom, and one day, when the king and queen and their little daughter came to visit the bakery, Molly made a present of her golden ball to the princess.

After that, Molly spent her time with her new dog, whom she called Prince. He was gentle and loyal, and he never complained about a thing. She still had to help out around the bakery, but it was much nicer. And it could be said that Molly got her happily ever after after all, for she found her prince, and they lived together, very happily, indeed. Prince never spoke a single word, but he was the best of friends, and every night, Molly would let him sleep on her bed.

# Mr. Fox and the Geese

**M**r. Fox liked to walk along the edge of the old city. One spring evening, he was strolling along, and he happened upon a marshy place where a flock of geese were gathered, splashing and gabbling in the swampy water.

"What do we have here?" he said, eyeing the fat geese, as he leaned on his walking cane. "Looks like dinner."

The geese were terrified, and they honked and cried for mercy.

"Mercy," laughed Mr. Fox. "You will find no mercy here. I'm interested in some dinner. Now you just line yourselves up in a row, and I will wring your pretty necks one by one, and then I'll take your carcasses back to my house in the city."

But there was one old goose who was at least as cunning as Mr. Fox. She was a grandam of the flock, and she peered up at Mr. Fox.

"Mr. Fox," she said, bobbing her head, "since you are going to eat us anyway, I don't suppose you would mind if I told my children and grandchildren one more story?"

Now, if Mr. Fox had a weakness, besides a greedy desire for fresh goose, it was for a good story. "Oh, very well," he said, petulantly. "Tell your story. But when you are done, I expect you to line up like good little geese so I can pick out the fattest for my table."

The old goose began her story. She gabbled and honked, telling of faraway places, of all the things she had seen on her travels, of the lives of people and animals, of strange and secret things only seen by moonlight and starlight. And before she was finished, she was joined by one of her children, and together, they gabbled and grumbled and honked of the places they had seen together. They were joined by the others, one by one, until soon the whole flock was gabbling the story of their travels, from the hot countries of the south to the wide spaces of the north.

The sun slowly set, and Mr. Fox listened, forgetting about everything else as he was swept away to places he had never known.

Did Mr. Fox ever get his dinner? Who can say?—for the geese are still telling their story to this day. And if you stop to listen, in the spring and the fall, you can hear it too—the gabbling of travelers' tales upon the air.

## Rapunzel, Not All That Tangled

The worst thing about being stuck in a tower, thought Rapunzel, was the boredom. She spent her days reading and gazing out the tower window. It got tedious.

Rapunzel was never entirely clear why she couldn't leave the tower. The old woman had explained it to her once. It was some muddled story about her parents and some lettuce—or was it a cabbage? She couldn't exactly remember. Whatever the reason, here she was, stuck in this tower, reading her books and looking out over the forest.

The old woman came to see her sometimes. When she did, she would stand at the foot of the tower and call, "Rapunzel, Rapunzel, let down your golden hair."

Rapunzel didn't understand why the old woman had to shout every time she came to the tower. She was usually at the window already. Rapunzel would let down her hair that reached right to the ground, and the old woman would climb up, carrying food or books or new clothes. They would always talk for a while, and the old woman would always warn Rapunzel about letting anyone into the tower.

As if she would! Rapunzel might be stuck in a tower, but she wasn't an idiot.

She supposed the old woman was talking about the young man she sometimes saw from her window. He would sneak out of the forest when the old woman wasn't there, come to the tower, and call, "Rapunzel, Rapunzel, let down your hair."

Good luck, buddy.

He couldn't have been the brightest crayon in the box if he thought she was just going to drop her braid out the window for anyone. And besides, gathering up all that hair was hard work, and she had to wash it every time the old woman used it as a climbing rope. And then she had to dry and braid it.

It went on like that, day after day, until, one day, Rapunzel decided she'd had enough. Towers were fine, but this was ridiculous. One of the books she had been reading was about a man who lived for years and years on a deserted island. He had to do all kinds of inventive things to survive on that island, and Rapunzel thought she would take a leaf out of his book—not literally, of course, but she liked some of his ideas.

She gathered up all that hair, masses and masses of it, and, taking a pair of scissors, she cut it off. With nimble fingers, Rapunzel began to weave herself a rope. Soon she had a golden rope that reached right down to the ground, and she wove the rest of the hair into another rope, which she stuffed into a makeshift bag she stitched from an old cloak. She took the heavy velvet dresses the old woman always made her wear, and she cut and stitched and stitched and cut. Soon she had a sensible set of clothes—pants, shirt, and jacket. Shoes were a problem, but Rapunzel rummaged through the pile of things at the back of the tower room until she unearthed a pair of combat boots the old woman had left by accident.

She was finally ready.

Saying a quick good-bye to the room, Rapunzel hopped out the window and rappelled down the side of the tower. It was wonderful to be outside, under her own steam, and finally able to do what she wanted.

She ventured into the forest, and there she built a house, following the example of her island survivor guy. She caught fish in a nearby lake, and she gathered edible plants from the forest. She was very happy.

Things went on for a while until, one evening, Rapunzel heard a bellowing and crashing in the forest. She caught up her walking stick, which also served as a beating stick, in case anyone should bother her, and she waited.

And guess who it was—the prince. He was crying and bellowing and crashing through the trees, not seeming to know where he was going, and Rapunzel felt a little sorry for him. She guided him into her little house and sat him down. He seemed to have something stuck in his eye.

"I saw the hair," he blubbered. "I saw the hair and thought you'd left it out for me. I tried climbing the tower, but I lost my grip and fell. I nearly broke my neck, and I got something stuck in my eye. I think it's a thorn from one of those beastly roses. I'm probably blind now!"

"Don't worry," said Rapunzel. "Just sit still and let me have a look."

And she had a look, but it was only an eyelash that had gotten stuck in the prince's eye. With one deft flick, Rapunzel got it out. "There you go," she said.

The prince sprang to his feet. "Rapunzel," he cried, "will you marry me and come and live as my wife in my castle?"

Rapunzel didn't have to consider long. "You realize I've been stuck in a tower for a long time," she said. "I don't think I want to be stuck in a castle. It sounds as bad as the tower."

"Oh," said the prince, looking crestfallen and a little hurt.

"But," said Rapunzel, brightly, "I'm off soon to see the world, and you are welcome to join me, if you like."

"Off to see the world?" said the prince, uncertainly.

"Yes, I have a list of places I want to visit. I want to see Stonehenge. I want to go to Brazil—I've always liked the nuts. I want to go to Canada, although they say it's always winter there, and I want to visit New Zealand. I've always wanted to visit New Zealand."

"I guess that would be fine," said the prince, a little uncertainly. "I should really ask my mother first."

And speaking of mothers, or at least old women, Rapunzel wanted to give hers a proper telling off before she went away. The old woman was contrite, and she begged Rapunzel's forgiveness, recognizing that imprisoning young girls in towers wasn't cool. And the old woman, whom some called a witch, went off and set up shop as a family therapist.

As for Rapunzel and the prince, they left to see the world. They visited Stonehenge, and they sailed on a ship to Canada. It wasn't always winter, but there were lots of mosquitoes. Next, they went to Brazil to eat nuts, and, finally, off to New Zealand. They toured around the North and South Islands, until they got an apartment in the city. It was in a high-rise. Rapunzel supposed it was part of her thing about towers. But she could leave this one whenever she wanted. You could say that she and the prince lived happily ever after, but Rapunzel forever kept her hair short.

## Sleeping Beauty, or How to Lose Your Fashion Blog

Once upon a time, there was a king and queen who wanted a child, ever so much. But they knew that raising a child meant work, so they began to prepare. They read books on childrearing, they baby proofed the castle, and they spent hours talking about names, immunizations, breastfeeding, and cloth diapers versus disposable.

And just as babies do, this baby came, and it was a girl. They called her Francesca, or Frankie for short. The king and queen began to organize the child's christening, and the king was put in charge of the guest list. Now, in the king's defense, he put thought and care into that list. He had names on colored sticky notes all over the royal study, and he gathered those names into a master list that he carried around in his pocket. He remembered to invite the seven dwarfs, the seven ravens, and every other king, queen, prince, or princess within a hundred miles. But when he added the names of the seven fairies to his list, he forgot one. And when the seventh fairy realized that she wasn't going to get an invitation, she was pretty mad.

The day of the christening came, the guests were gathered, and all went off without a hitch—almost. The king was walking about the castle gardens where the christening was held, and little Frankie was snoodled up in a snuggly strapped to his chest. He beamed upon all of his guests, wandering about and shaking hands, while the queen wished it all would be over soon. She needed a nap. One by one, the guests presented their gifts to the new princess.

Just then, the seventh, and conspicuously uninvited, fairy arrived at the garden. She was dressed in a black Armani suit, and she looked foreboding. Not only was she a powerful fairy, she was one of the top fashion bloggers in that part of the world.

As soon as he spotted her, the king realized his mistake. To his credit, he hurried over to offer an apology, but the seventh fairy wouldn't have it.

"I'm not interested in your excuses, you old windbag," she said coldly. "Here is my gift to your little brat of a child." And with that, she put a curse on the princess. "When this child reaches the age of sixteen years," the fairy intoned, "she will prick her finger on a spindle, which will put her to sleep for a hundred years, unless a prince wakes her with a kiss."

"Oh," she added quickly, "if a prince does kiss her, and if she wakes up, she will forever lack a fashion sense."

A shocked silence followed the words of the fairy, and then a cry of dismay. The king begged the fairy to take back her cruel words and have some punch, but she shook her head.

"You must face the consequences of your forgetfulness," she said to the king.

"But you were on my list," wailed the king. "Can't you forgive me? For the sake of my poor little daughter?"

"Not a chance," said the fairy, and with that, she turned on her glittering spiked heel and left the party.

You can imagine the dismay of the king and queen. "What are we going to do?" cried the queen.

"And never to have a fashion sense!" added one of the ladies-in-waiting, one hand to her aching brow.

"Now, now, my queen," said the king, recovering his dignity. "We will take steps, we will prepare, and we will stop this vile curse from ever coming to pass."

So little Frankie began to grow. She became a toddler, and then a sturdy child, and soon a long-legged girl, who ran and laughed and made noise and got herself into trouble. She had hair as black as the raven's wing and eyes as blue as a summer's day. She laughed often and freely, and she tried the patience of her parents. She hated wearing princess clothes and would most often be seen, whether in the kitchen talking to the cooks or in the yard chasing the stable-boys, wearing an old black T-shirt and jeans.

"Part of the curse is already coming true," whispered the ladies-in-waiting to one another. "The princess Francesca has no fashion sense."

But Frankie didn't care, and her parents had more to worry about as the princess approached her sixteenth birthday.

The king had done his part by rounding up all of the spindles in the kingdom and making a great bonfire that could be seen for a hundred miles. Next, he advertised for a prince—the kissing kind—just in case things went sideways on Frankie's birthday. There must have been many princes wandering the lands that year, because at least fifty showed up at the palace to be on hand in case the princess fell into an enchanted sleep. But the king wasn't going to take any chances, and he housed them all, letting them practice their princely skills on the royal training ground. Frankie would sometimes go and watch them. She liked sports as much as anyone else, but she wasn't about to join this posturing collection of fools, just so they could try and show her up. She left them to their swordplay, their archery, and their flexing.

The princess's sixteenth birthday drew nearer and nearer, and the kingdom seemed to hold its breath. And then, the morning of Frankie's birthday arrived.

Perhaps not so surprisingly, the king and queen couldn't find their daughter that morning. Frankie had risen early, and on her way down to the kitchens, she discovered a stairway into a tower that she had never noticed before.

"How odd," she said to herself. And being the curious girl she was, she followed the stairs, up and up, until she came to a tower room. And there, as you probably guessed, sat an old woman with a spindle in her hands. She grinned crookedly as Frankie entered the tower room.

"Good morning, my sweet," said the old woman in honeyed tones.

"Hello," said Frankie. "What is it you are doing?"

"I'm spinning, my dear. Would you like to try?"

Now, Frankie wasn't as stupid as all that. For one thing, she had heard the story of what was supposed to happen on her sixteenth birthday a hundred times. Everyone had always made a fuss about it, and now, here was this old woman, clearly trying to set Frankie up for her big sleep.

"All right," said Frankie, coming close. "But first show me what to do."

"Very well," said the seventh fairy, for it was she in the disguise of an old woman. "Watch carefully." And she showed Frankie how to spin the spindle and wrap the wool.

Frankie came closer, as though she was trying to see what the old woman was doing, and she just happened to bump the old woman's arm.

The old woman gave a cry. "Clumsy child!" she shrieked. "What have you done?" She held up her finger. Right at the tip was a bright bead of blood.

"Oops," said Frankie.

The old woman turned pale, and then she turned green, and then she lost her disguise completely, and the seventh fairy, in all her radiant beauty, fell over with a crash onto the floor—sound asleep.

Frankie regarded her for a moment. Another princess might have left the fairy to her long sleep, but Frankie wasn't so cruel. She headed down the stairs and out onto the training ground. She walked up to the first likely looking prince she saw.

"There's a beautiful lady inside the castle who is under an enchanted sleep. Want to come and give her a kiss?"

"But of course," cried the prince, slapping a ham-like hand to his chest. "It is my destiny, my duty, my honor."

And with that, he followed Frankie back into the castle and up the stairs. When he saw the fairy lying on the floor beside the fallen spindle, he went down onto his knees. "My dear, enchanted lady," he murmured. And then he bent down and kissed her gently on the lips.

The eyes of the fairy flew open. She looked at the face of the prince above her, and then she looked at Frankie. "What. Have. You. Done?" she asked in measured tones.

"Just giving you a taste of your own medicine," said Frankie coolly. "You actually haven't been asleep long, and look, you now have your very own prince. As for your fashion sense, I'm less sure about that."

"My blog?" shrieked the fairy. "I'll be ruined! What will I do?"

"You'll be fine," said Frankie, and she skipped off down the stairs.

When the king and queen heard what happened, they were much relieved. The king announced a feast to celebrate Frankie's sixteenth birthday, and he promised never again to give her a hard time about running riot all over the castle. This time, the king remembered to invite the seventh fairy, but by that time, she was already half a kingdom away, with her faithful prince in tow, and fated never to blog again.

As for Frankie, she enjoyed her party, and she went on with her life. She was, after all, only sixteen years old. She started to think of a career. Maybe curse breaker, she thought. But, really, she had plenty of time to consider.

## Snow White, or Learning to Love Your Stepmother

Once a queen sat sewing by a window. She longed for a child. As she looked out over the snowy landscape, she saw a raven. She started and pricked her finger with the needle, so a drop of blood fell upon the sill.

She thought, if I had a child whose skin was white as snow, whose lips were as red as blood, and whose hair was as black as a raven's wing, then I would call her Snow White.

She did have a child, but she didn't live to watch her daughter grow up. In memory of his wife, the king named the child Snow White. It was a ridiculous name, because the child's hair was red as red, and she had so many freckles it was hard to tell one from another.

But the king didn't care, and he went off to mourn his dead wife. The only trouble with mourning someone for years and years—as kings in fairy tales so often do—is that they miss the stuff going on right under their noses, as this king did. He took hardly any notice of Snow White.

As for the child, she hated the name Snow White, and she insisted that all of the servants call her Rocky. No one ever knew exactly why Snow White insisted on her nickname, but neither was anyone willing to argue with her. If they did, Rocky would fly into a temper and stamp her feet.

Rocky wasn't a bad child, but she did get her way more than she should have. And even if she was loud, she eventually saw the justice in every situation. The old cook, who was like a second mother to the princess, and the only person Rocky ever heeded, did her best to raise the child and teach her right from wrong.

So it went until the king brought home a new wife. When the royal coach rolled up to the front gate, the whole castle held its breath. They all waited to see if Rocky would fly into a temper. But as the king and the new queen came up the steps and entered the great hall, Rocky just watched, a strange expression on her face.

Rocky was just seven years old, and she didn't know much about kings and queens and marriage, but she knew that she had already lost her mother, and now she was losing her father for the second time.

The new queen settled into the castle, and soon she was bossing everyone around and making herself unpopular with the servants. She didn't like her food, and she complained about the drafty castle. The fires were too hot or too low. And Rocky, no matter what, was always in the way. Rocky felt a little sorry for herself, but it didn't last.

The worst of it was the mirrors. The queen placed them at strategic points all over the castle, and she was always checking her reflection. No matter what she did, the queen always had one eye on a mirror, checking to see that she was at her best.

It was weird. It's like she's her own audience, thought Rocky.

One day, thinking to play a trick on her stepmother, Rocky let herself into the queen's apartments. She sneaked over to the tall mirror, and she wondered if she could do something to the mirror so the queen would look fat. One of the coachmen had told Rocky about a fair in the town where you could stand in front of a mirror that made you look tall and thin or short and wide. Just then, the handle of the door clicked, and Rocky knew it was time to hide. Quick as a flash, she jumped behind the mirror and waited.

The queen swept into her apartments, checking her entrance in one of the wall mirrors. She spent a long time at her bureau touching up her makeup and peering at the effect. She had a smaller mirror for this purpose. Each time Rocky peeped from behind the tall mirror in the corner, the queen was dabbing at another part of her face.

Finally, the queen wandered languidly over to the mirror where Rocky hid. "Oh, mirror," said the queen. "If you could only tell me I'm the fairest in all the land, then I would at least hear what I know to be true."

Rocky had an idea. She caught up a tall, glass vase that lay discarded near the mirror. "Oh, queen," she said, speaking into the tall vase. It made her voice sound spooky and weird. "You are the fairest in all the land, save for the lovely Snow White."

This time, when she peeped out from behind the glass, the queen was glaring at the mirror. "Snow White!" she nearly shrieked. "How can that ragged child even compare to me? Perish the thought."

The queen began pacing up and down her room. "This is ridiculous," she said to herself. "I must do something." And she struck a pose in the center of the room. Then she sent for the royal huntsman.

Now, the royal huntsman was Rocky's friend. They had spent many an hour together, making s'mores over the great fire in the kitchen, while the huntsman told her stories about his adventures in the forest. When he arrived at the queen's apartments, Rocky thought he looked a little confused.

"Huntsman," cried the queen, "I have a job for you."

"Yes, my lady," said the huntsman, bowing his head.

"I want you to take Snow White into the forest and dispose of her."

"Dispose," said the huntsman, looking blankly at the queen, "of Snow White?"

"Yes," said the queen. "Dispose of her in any way you see fit. Drown her in a pool or feed her to a wild beast. I don't care. Just get rid of her." The queen had certainly heard of such things in stories, and it seemed the best way.

The huntsman stood for a moment. "Yes, my queen," he said finally. But he had no intention of getting rid of Snow White. Was the queen mad? He had half a mind to go straight to the king, but the huntsman thought better of it. He headed to the kitchen to talk to the cook.

In the meantime, Rocky waited for her chance, and then she slipped out of the queen's chambers. So, she thought to herself, my stepmother wants to dispose of me. We'll see about that. She pelted off to her own room. She filled a backpack with things that would help her on a journey, put on her heavy coat and shoes, and then slipped out the back door of the castle and headed into the forest.

Rocky walked through the forest all night. It was dark, close, and scary. Even Rocky, who wasn't afraid of much, soon began to get unnerved by the shadows and the silence. She had walked as far as she could when she came upon a little house. It was neat and snug, and it sat there in the middle of a small clearing, just as though a giant hand had set it down like a toy.

Rocky didn't care if anyone was inside; she wanted to get out of the trees for a while. She cracked open the little door and sneaked inside.

She had just closed the door when she heard such a racket that she nearly wanted to run. The snoring, sighing, and belching that filled the little house made Rocky wonder if she had wandered into a den of bears. But, no. With the light of dawn through the windows, Rocky saw seven beds lined up against the wall, and in each bed was a form, snoring and blowing and muttering.

Rocky hid herself as best she could. It wasn't long before one of the figures got up and began tending the fire in the stove. Soon, the little house was filled with the smells of fresh coffee and oatmeal porridge flavored with cinnamon. Rocky's stomach growled.

When Rocky peeped out from behind the barrel where she hid, she could see that all the little men were now sitting around the table, slurping coffee, shoveling in porridge, and handing around a plate of scones. They were dwarfs, with shaggy hair and long beards.

"Brothers," said one of the dwarfs, "I think an animal has broken into our house."

The others looked at him and nodded. "Indeed," said another.

"Is it a monster?" said a third.

"Or a forest demon?" said a fourth.

"Or perhaps," said the first, "it is a naughty princess who has run away from the castle."

"Surely not," cried the others.

Rocky sighed. "All right," she said, coming out from behind the barrel. "I'm right here."

The dwarfs all gave a convincing jump. "The monster!" cried one. "The demon!" cried another.

"I'm sorry I sneaked into your house," said Rocky, with all of the dignity of a small princess. "But could I please have some breakfast? I've been wandering around the forest all night."

Laughing, the dwarfs made room for her at the table. Soon Rocky had a steaming bowl of oatmeal, a hot scone, and a mug of coffee. It was delicious.

The dwarfs, of course, wanted to know her story, but they waited until Rocky had eaten her fill. Then she told them about the queen.

"A bad business," said one, shaking his shaggy head.

"You can stay here with us," said another, "at least until you get this all sorted out." The other dwarfs nodded.

"I'm never going back," said Rocky, now near to tears. But it had been a long night, and she was, after all, only seven.

One of the dwarfs made her a bed in the corner, and soon Rocky was tucked up and falling asleep. The dwarfs got ready for their day in the mines, but one agreed to stay behind—to mind the princess. He got his knitting and sat on a chair in the morning sun, while Rocky slept.

Meanwhile, the night before, the huntsman had gone to see the old cook. But even before he came storming into the kitchen, the whole castle already knew the princess had run away. "Do you know what that woman asked me?" thundered the huntsman, as soon as he stood before the cook.

Everyone knew who that woman was. "I can guess," said the old cook, while the undercooks and serving lads and lasses stopped to listen.

The huntsman told his tale. "And now the princess has run off into the forest. What are we to do?"

The old cook looked thoughtful. "First," she said, "you needn't worry about the princess. She'll be safe. She'll find her way to the house of the seven dwarfs. You can check on her in the morning, if you like. I will deal with the queen tomorrow."

The next morning, the huntsman left for the forest, and soon enough he came to the house of the dwarfs. It wasn't that far from the castle. Rocky had been going in rather a circle the night before. The huntsman found one of the dwarfs seated on a chair, his knitting needles clicking and flashing in the sun.

"Come for your princess?" asked the dwarf, glancing up at the huntsman. "She's fast asleep inside. Help yourself to coffee."

The huntsman knew the dwarfs well. He was relieved, to say the least. He had a quick look at the sleeping princess, and then he took a chair and a cup of coffee and joined the dwarf outside.

Back at the castle, everyone knew what had happened the night before. There was some angry muttering, but the old cook said that she would take care of the queen. The cook was a wise woman, and she had a little magic of her own. Taking a small looking glass from her pocket, she peered into its murky depths. She spoke to it. It flashed once and went dim again. With a little smile, the old cook tucked the mirror back into her pocket, and then she went to check the bread that had just come out of the ovens.

It was the queen's custom to sleep late. The king had left early with a hunting party, and the morning was well underway when suddenly the whole castle heard a shriek.

"The queen's awake," said the old cook.

The shriek was soon followed by another, and soon a wailing and blubbering queen came down the steps. "My mirrors!" she screamed. "What has happened to my mirrors? They're all broken!"

It was true. Every mirror in the castle was covered with a spider web of cracks, and they were all as dull as the winter sky.

The old cook let it go on for a while, and then she went to look for the queen. The woman was slumped on a chair in the great hall. The cook stood before the queen. "Your Highness," she said, "you have done an unconscionable thing."

The queen looked up at the cook through her tears. She wasn't especially good at listening to others, but something in the cook's tone made her pay attention.

"What have I done?" she sobbed. "Some wicked person has broken all of my mirrors."

"You only got what you deserved," said the cook, "after what you tried to do to the princess."

"The princess," said the queen. And since she didn't have a mirror to distract her, the queen had to think for a moment.

"Yes, the princess. You should be ashamed of yourself. What sort of queen asks the royal huntsman to dispose of a little girl?"

The queen wasn't a bad sort, really. She was vain, and she read too many fairy tales, but she didn't actually mean Rocky any harm.

"If you do the right thing," said the old cook, "maybe—just maybe—one or two of these mirrors will start working again."

The queen sniffed. "If you mean," she said, with another sniff, "that I should apologize, then I suppose I could. Then I can have my mirrors back?" She looked hopefully up at the cook.

"You'll have to do better than that," said the cook, glowering down.

"Very well! I suppose I haven't been a good stepmother, so I'll do my best to be a better one to dear little Snow White."

"And?"

"And what?" cried the queen.

"It will be hard acting like a stepmother if all you're doing is looking in the mirror."

"I'll keep my mirrors in my room," sulked the queen.

The old cook could see she wasn't going to get much better than that, so she let it be. She called for a footman, who escorted the queen into the forest and to the house of the seven dwarfs. There, in front of all the dwarfs, the huntsman, and the footman, the queen apologized to Rocky.

Rocky stood awhile, and then she said, "You should know that it was me hiding behind your mirror yesterday. It wasn't your mirror talking. It was me. I wanted to play a trick on you. I'm sorry, too."

The dwarfs and the two men held their breaths as they watched the little princess and the tall queen, who looked hard at one another.

"Well," said the queen, finally, "if you promise not to do anything of the sort again, I will do my best as your stepmother."

Rocky gave a reluctant grin. "All right," she said, and, taking her stepmother's hand, she led her back to the castle.

There was a great feast that night, and the seven dwarfs were invited to stay at the castle. The king smiled absently as he greeted everyone, but he wasn't sure what had happened that day. And since finding out would have meant taking an interest, he didn't bother.

Rocky and her stepmother sat side by side at the great table, while the seven dwarfs drank and made merry around them. "We'll have to do something about your father, next," said the queen.

And Rocky nodded her head. "Good idea," she said.

# The Bronze Egg, a Fairy Tale

Once upon a time, an old man lay dying in his bedchamber. His three sons sat near. Of the three, the youngest loved his father the best, and he sat at the end of the bed while the tears rolled down his cheeks.

It wasn't as though the two elder sons did not love their father. But they were both practical minded, and they recognized that their father's time had simply come. The old man was also rich, and they both looked forward to their inheritance, the thought of the old man's gold eating at the edges of their hearts as they sat through the long night.

The old man was weak, but finally he opened his eyes and spoke to his sons.

"My dear sons," he said. "My time has indeed come. I love you all, and I have left each of you something to help you in your lives ahead. Remember that the gift that I leave each of you will allow you to show your love not just for me, but for one another. Use my gifts well."

"Yes, father," cried the older brothers together. "We will."

"But where," said the oldest, "have you left these gifts for us, Father?"

"They are in the east wing of the house," said the old man in his weak voice. "Once I am dead, each of you can go and claim his inheritance." And then the old man fell back onto his pillows and did not speak again, and the three sons sat on as the old man's labored breathing continued on through the darkening night.

Strange things can enter the heart during such a vigil. And it was at the darkest hour of the night when the oldest brother slipped out of the bedchamber and headed for the east wing of the house.

He crept along, carrying a dark lantern in one hand. At last, he came to the first of three closed doors in the east wing of the house.

The oldest brother opened the door and peered inside. Sitting in the middle of the floor was a great chest. The eldest son hurried into the room and threw back the lid of the chest. Inside lay more gold than he had ever seen, and his heart leaped.

As quickly and quietly as he could, the eldest son found some sacks and began filling them with the gold. When the bags were full, he crept out of the house and away, not bothering to take anything with him. For now I am richer than I ever dreamed, thought the eldest brother. I can buy anything I want or need. And, his heart pounding with joy and greed, he hurried away into the night.

The second brother had, of course, noticed that the eldest had slipped away. He knew very well where his brother was going. The second waited long enough to make sure the younger brother had fallen asleep, and then he too slipped out of the old man's bedchamber.

The night had begun to grow old as the second brother crept through the house toward the east wing. He came to the first room and found it empty. Ha! thought he. My brother has been here and taken his inheritance. I will feel less badly taking what is mine and leaving that fool of a youngest brother to find what he may.

And with that, the second brother crept along the hall until he came to the second door. He opened the door to find a chest standing in the middle of the room. He opened the chest and found glittering stones—diamonds, rubies, and emeralds—more wealth than he had ever imagined. He too filled some sacks, and he hurried off into the night, just like his elder brother.

As dawn was beginning to lighten the horizon, the elder brother found himself at the edge of a river. He peered into the darkness at the water. "It can't be that deep," he said to himself. And he began wading out into the shadowy river. It wasn't long before he came to the middle of the river, and he began to hurry, thinking he was almost out and safe, when he caught his foot on a stone and slipped.

The current was strong, even if the river wasn't especially deep. But the eldest was intent on hanging onto the sacks of gold. But they were so heavy that they dragged him down. He was swept into a deeper part of the river, and there he drowned, never wanting to let go of his gold.

Meanwhile, the second brother had taken a different path upon leaving the house of his father. He followed a road through the night until he came to a crossroad. The sky was streaked with dawn as he stopped to catch his breath. The sacks of jewels were heavy. As he stood, wondering what way to take, robbers leaped out on every side.

"Well, what have we here?" said the chief bandit.

Full of fear, the second brother tried to run with his sacks of wealth, but the robbers cut him down with swords. They laughed with delight when they opened the bags to find the diamonds and rubies and emeralds. They cast the body of the second brother into the forest, and they took up the sacks and disappeared into the forest, back to their hideout.

The sun was just rising when the youngest brother woke with a start to find his brothers gone and his father lying dead in his bed.

The youngest son wept over the body of his father, and then he covered the old man's face and went to find the priest.

The priest came, and the neighbors came. And they grieved for the old man, for he was a good-hearted and generous man, and all loved him.

When the old man was buried in the church-yard and the neighbors all gone home, the youngest brother sat by the fire, thinking of his father and feeling the silence of the great house all around him. The silence got him thinking about what had happened to his brothers, and that got him thinking about his father's words of the inheritance. Curious to know about his brothers as much as about his own inheri-tance, the youngest brother took a lantern and climbed the stairs to the east wing.

He came to the first room and found an empty chest. He came to the second room and found there an empty chest. He came to the third room, and there he found another chest.

Stepping curiously up to the chest, he lifted the lid. Inside, lying at the bottom, was what looked like an egg. He took it carefully up, and it shone dully in the light from his lantern. It was heavy in his hand, and he carried it downstairs to his seat by the fire.

Sitting by the fire, he could see that it was a bronze egg.

"Why would my father leave me such a gift?" he wondered aloud. But he didn't care, and he wrapped the egg lovingly in a cloth and stowed it into a pocket near his heart.

The next day, the youngest son set out to find his brothers. He walked and walked until he came to a river. On the edge of the river stood a little man—a dwarf, dressed in sackcloth and peering at the youngest son with beady eyes.

"You come seeking your brothers," said the dwarf.

"Yes," said the youngest son. "And how did you know?"

The dwarf ignored the question. "If you give me the thing that lies closest to your heart, I will tell you where to find your brother."

The youngest had to think about it for a moment. The thing closest to his heart was the bronze egg given him by his father. He didn't want to give up the egg, but he thought his father would want him to find his brothers.

He drew the egg from his pocket and wordlessly handed it over to the dwarf.

"Look in the river," said the little man. "You will find your brother and his inheritance."

The youngest brother didn't understand, but he stepped down to the bank of the river and began to wade into the water. At a deeper point in the river, he found his brother, held down by three great heavy sacks. The youngest brother dragged the body out of the river along with the sacks. He hailed a boy driving a donkey cart and took his brother home, making sure to give the boy one of the gold coins he found in the sacks.

The youngest son called the priest, but this time no one came to mourn with the youngest son. He sat on by the fire until he fell asleep.

He had a dream as he slept, and he dreamed of his father. "You have done well, my son," said his father. "You have brought back your brother, but now you must seek my second son. Bring him home to lie next to his brother."

When the youngest son woke, he found his hand clutching the bronze egg.

It was the strangest thing. But the youngest did not question his dream. He found his coat, and he ventured out in the night that was now lightening toward dawn.

The youngest brother had no idea where to look, but he followed the road until he came to a fork. There stood an old woman as though waiting for him.

"You seek your elder brother," she said in a voice that creaked like an old gate.

"Yes," said the youngest brother. "He disappeared from our father's deathbed two nights ago."

"I can tell you what befell your brother, but you must give me that which lies nearest to your heart."

The youngest brother thought at once of the bronze egg, and this time he did not hesitate. He took the egg from his breast pocket, and he handed it to the old woman, this time thinking he would for certain never see it again.

The old woman pocketed the egg at once. "If you follow this road into the forest, you will find him and his inheritance. But you must be brave, for your brother has been murdered by a band of robbers. It is they who have his inheritance."

And with that, the old woman was gone.

"Robbers," said the youngest brother to himself. "How am I to get back my father's treasure from robbers?"

But he took a deep breath, and he followed the road until he came to a place overshadowed by trees. He left the road and walked into the forest.

It wasn't long before he came upon a broken-down shack among the trees. The youngest stepped up to the door, which was hanging crookedly, and he peered inside.

There were the robbers, all asleep with their heads on their arms. And the youngest brother could see the empty cups and flagons scattered over the table.

They must have been celebrating their good fortune, thought the youngest brother.

And he stepped quickly inside, and he found three great sacks that he knew must be his father's treasure. He took up the sacks, and he left as quietly as he had come.

It was when he came back to the road that he found his brother's body. And then his heart sank, for his father had wanted him to return with his brother's body.

He was about to abandon the sacks when he heard the crunch and roll of wheels on the road. He peered out from the trees to see a man driving a cart with a high-stepping horse out in front. He begged the man to help him with his brother's body.

The man, who was a merchant, had heard about bandits in that part of the forest, but he could see by the youngest brother's face that he was an honest lad. He helped the youngest brother with the body of his brother. They tossed the sacks into the back, and then they drove back to town.

Once the merchant knew who the youngest brother was, he became much friendlier. "I knew your father, lad," he said. "And I was sad to hear of his passing, and I will do all I can to help you in his memory."

The youngest brother thanked the merchant, and when they came back to the front doors of his father's house, the youngest brother handed the merchant a diamond from one of the sacks.

The merchant's eyes widened. "You are as generous as your father," he cried. "Bless you, young master."

And it seemed as though the youngest brother was blessed, although he didn't feel it for some time to come.

That afternoon, he buried the third family member in three days. The priest came once again, but no one else. And that evening, once again, the youngest brother found himself sitting and nodding by the fire.

He dreamed again that night, and his father came to him, smiling, and saying, "You are indeed my son. I give you my blessing, and I would only ask that you remain as selfless and generous in spirit as you have shown yourself these past days." And then the dream faded, and the youngest slept deeply.

After that, the youngest brother was indeed blessed. He set his mind to helping those in need. He learned to run his father's farm and his father's business so well that he was never short of gold.

He became as famous for his good deeds as his father. And when he fell in love with a pretty girl from the village, there was a wedding at the old house, and it was once again filled with laughter and merriment. And in the years to come, the youngest brother, who was now an important merchant farmer of the countryside, had sons and daughters of his own. And he loved them all, and the old house echoed with their talk and laughter.

And sometimes, during the long nights of winter, his children would climb over him as he and his pretty wife sat by the fire. They would beg him to tell them tales, to tell them about things past and things present, but their favorite of all was the story of the bronze egg.

# The Seven Ravens, or How to Rescue Your Brothers

Once upon a time in the old city lived a man, his wife, and their seven sons. The sons were all big, strapping boys, and they worked hard for their father in the machine shop that lay on the edge of town. The father and his sons repaired small appliances and old cars, but the place was half a junkyard. They collected the stuff people didn't want, and they either repaired it or sold it, or they tore it apart for bits that might be useful in fixing other things.

The father and his wife were content, but those seven sons did sometimes make them long for a daughter. And one day, it happened. The wife gave birth to a beautiful daughter, and they called her Margaret, for her grandmother. If the mother and father were content with their new daughter, the seven brothers were ecstatic.

Now Margaret, or Maggie, as the family loved to call her, was a sickly child, and her parents feared that she wouldn't live past her first birthday.

"No child of mine will die unbaptized," cried the father. And he got on the phone to the priest, and he arranged for the man to come out to the shop to baptize Maggie. In preparation for the day, the father sent his seven sons to fetch the water for the baptism.

"There is a spring outside the city," said the father to his eldest son. "It's the cleanest water you will find. Go to the spring with your brothers and bring back enough water to properly baptize your sister. Take one of the small tubs, and fill it full."

The seven sons practically fell over one another in their eagerness to get out of the city and find the spring. It only took two of them to carry the empty tub, and they took turns hauling it along. They were good boys, but they didn't always listen carefully enough to their father. They argued back and forth as they walked, none of them very clear as to where they were going, and soon they were lost.

Finally, in the late afternoon and as the sun was beginning to set, they came upon the spring. "Here it is!" cried the eldest.

"Sweet!" cried the others.

And they were so eager to dip out a tub full of water that the second eldest, who had the end closest to the edge of the deep spring, lost his grip, and with a splash the tub fell into the spring. It floated there for a moment, and then it sank like a rock.

"Aw, crap!" cried the eldest, looking disbelievingly at the water.

"Nice move, butterfingers," said the youngest to the second eldest.

"What are we going to do now?" asked the second youngest.

"We'll have to fish it out," said the second eldest.

"You mean, you will have to fish it out," said the youngest.

"Dad is going to kill us," said the eldest.

They tried and tried, but the pool was deep, and by the time it was dark, they were huddled together, soaking wet and shivering at the edge of the spring.

"Dad's going to kill us," said the eldest again through chattering teeth.

The father, of course, didn't know what was taking his sons so long, and he grew impatient. Then he did a stupid thing.

"Oh," he cried, "I wish those boys would all be turned into ravens, and I would be rid of them."

The father was angry, and he didn't really mean it, but no sooner had he spoken the words than his seven sons, who still sat huddled at the edge of the spring, suddenly transformed into great black, flapping ravens. They rose in the air as a group, and they flew away into the country.

Little Maggie got her baptism after all, and she soon grew strong and healthy. But her father, probably out of shame, never told her about her seven brothers. The father had to run the machine shop all by himself, but soon Maggie grew handy with a screwdriver and a drill. She could do just about anything her father could do.

Maggie was a smart girl, and she soon put together the story of her brothers' disappearance. The seven rooms on the second floor of the house that always remained locked were a bit of a clue, and no lock in the world could stop Maggie once she had decided to open it.

The day Maggie turned twelve, she confronted her parents. "What," she asked, "happened to my seven brothers?"

Her mother simply looked sad, but her father looked ashamed. He told Maggie the whole sorry tale. That night, Maggie decided it was time to get her brothers back. Buckling on her tool belt, Maggie set off, determined to bring her brothers home.

Maggie found her way out of the city, and she walked and walked and walked. After a time, she came to a hotel beside the road. Sunny Acres was written in large letters over the door, and Maggie let herself in. It was rather gloomy inside, in spite of the name above the door, and Maggie peered at a great, fat man who stood behind the counter. He was wearing a Bermuda shirt and shorts, and his sun hat was pulled low over his eyes.

"I'm looking for my seven brothers," said Maggie, not liking the look of the man at all.

"Brothers?" said the man. "Not sure if I can help you, missy, but why don't you come in and rest yourself from your travels?"

Maggie caught a glimpse of glowing, red eyes and flashing, sharp teeth, so she beat it out of there in a hurry.

She walked and walked until she came to another hotel—Moonlight Inn, read the sign.

Looks dodgy, thought Maggie to herself as she peered inside the double doors. She had a glimpse of people in white suits, wandering here and there, and snapping silvery teeth as they ate from little plates and drank something from silver goblets that looked remarkably like blood.

"I don't think so," said Maggie to herself, and clutching her best screwdriver tightly, she headed off down the road.

She walked and walked again, until she came to a third hotel—The Five Star, Star Hotel, said the sign. Oh, brother, thought Maggie.

Inside the hotel, stars of every variety were wandering about: TV stars, movie stars, and stars of the stage.

"A waif! How scrumptious!" cried one of the stars, spotting Maggie. "Come in, dear. Tell us your story."

Maggie came all of the way into the great lobby of the hotel, and soon she was surrounded by people with dazzling smiles, expensively coiffed hair, and designer clothes.

"I'm looking for my brothers," explained Maggie. And she told them the sorry tale.

"Darling, you are breaking my heart," said the first star, a tall woman with an elaborate dress and flashing diamond necklace. "She's so precious. Isn't she precious?" she said to the others, and they made sympathetic sounds of agreement.

"Can you help me?" asked Maggie.

"If I remember correctly," said the first star, "there is a casino just down the road run by seven brothers. I'm not sure if they're ravens," she said, pausing to give Maggie another dazzling smile, "but they do all dress in black—I think."

"Thank you," said Maggie. "That's very helpful."

"Oh, and here," said the woman. "Take this. You'll need a key card to get in." And she handed Maggie a plastic card.

Maggie tucked the card into her pocket and headed down the road once again. She didn't really need it, but anything might be helpful. It was getting late, and Maggie was starting to feel hungry. She walked and walked. By the time she came to the next town and found the casino, it was as dark as dark. Maggie stared up at the glass-fronted building. The place looked closed, but even in the darkness, Maggie could read above the great, double doors in fancy black letters, The Seven Ravens Casino.

Interesting, thought Maggie. Now, how do I get in?

She wandered around the side of the building until she came to a service door. It was metal and shut tight.

"Not to worry," said Maggie to herself. She took a pick from her tool belt, and in two minutes she had that door open.

Maggie crept inside. She followed a hallway until it came into a kitchen, all gleaming surfaces and hung with pots and pans. Then she came into a great hall. Directly across was another set of double doors that Maggie thought must lead into the casino itself.

"Hey, who are you?" cried a voice.

Maggie turned her head to see a dwarf wearing a tuxedo striding toward her.

"We're closed," said the dwarf, roughly. "How did you get in here?"

Maggie knew this was not the time for messing around. "I'm looking for my brothers. They were turned into ravens. I think they own this casino."

The dwarf halted, peering at her closely. "Good heavens," he said. "It's the sister!"

He seem to consider for a moment. "If you are indeed the sister, then you are the only one who can break the spell that lies upon my masters." He waved a hand. "Come with me," he said.

He led Maggie down a hall and into a smaller room. "Your brothers will return soon for their dinners," he said. "Wait here until they return. But if you want my advice, you'll hide yourself until you can turn them back into humans." And with that, he left Maggie to herself.

Maggie looked at the long table. It was set with seven plates and seven cups. She looked closer at each plate and nearly gagged, for the plates each held roadkill in varying stages of decay. She looked at the cups. They smelled marshy.

Suddenly, Maggie heard a ruckus from the great hall. Thinking quickly, Maggie took a bolt from her tool belt and dropped it into one of the cups. Then she hid herself behind a sideboard and waited.

Into the room came the seven ravens, squawking and flapping and croaking. Maggie pressed her hands to her ears—they were so loud.

They began to tear at the roadkill on their plates.

"Delicious," croaked one.

"A marvelous bouquet," squawked another, raising his glass to his beak. "But wait," he cried, dipping a claw into the cup. "What is this?"

All of the ravens stopped their tearing and feasting to look. "It's a bolt," said one.

"A bolt, indeed," said another. "It's very shiny."

"Oh, if it were but a sign from our dear sister," said a third. "If she were here to help us, this terrible spell would be broken."

That was Maggie's cue. She came out from behind the sideboard and stood before her brothers. And with a sizzling pop the spell was broken, and there sat her seven brothers, all looking a little bewildered, and one with a long piece of roadkill still dangling from his mouth. He spat it out. As a group, they stood up and began to cheer.

Maggie had never felt so pleased in her short life. Her brothers patted her back and hugged her tight until Maggie was nearly breathless. They praised her to the skies, and even though they could have, not one said anything bad about their father, who had caused the spell to be cast in the first place.

They called the dwarf and demanded that he prepare a proper feast of people food. The dwarf was pleased to see that his masters had returned to their human form, even though he had only ever known them as ravens. He got busy in the kitchen, and soon a feast was laid upon the table. Maggie ate and ate, which made her very sleepy. And soon, one of her brothers—she wasn't sure which one—picked her up and carried her off to a soft bed with warm blankets.

And that was the end of the story. Maggie wanted to go home, but not all of her brothers were willing. They were, after all, the successful owners of a casino. They promoted the dwarf, making him the concierge of the establishment. Five brothers decided to remain at the casino, while the eldest and the youngest decided to accompany Maggie back to the machine shop.

"I'm sure our father could use some extra help," said the eldest. "Not that we could be as helpful as you," he said, smiling at Maggie.

Everyone was pleased, even the dwarf, although his new position meant a good deal more work. And when Maggie returned home with two of her brothers, the reunion was joyful. And never again was the machine shop a quiet place.

## The Wedding of Mrs. Fox,
## That Didn't Actually Happen

**M**r. Fox lived with his wife in the old city. He insisted Mrs. Fox do all that was required of a good wife, but he was a lousy husband. He spent his time drinking, gambling, and trolling the streets of the city with his friend, Mr. Wolf. The two thought of one another as friends, but they generally didn't trust one another for a second.

One day, Mr. Fox decided to play a trick on his wife. He suspected her of cheating, and he was determined to catch her in the act. Coming home from a night of carousing with Mr. Wolf, Mr. Fox lay as though dead on the couch in the front room. And he waited.

Mrs. Fox came down at her usual time to make the coffee and set the bread to rise for the second time. She spotted her husband lying as though dead on the couch—tongue lolling and eyes half closed. What is he up to? she thought.

She stepped up to the couch and looked down. "Oh, mercy," she cried. "My poor husband is dead! What will become of me?"

She cried and wailed and wailed and cried until the ruckus brought Mrs. Mole scurrying from next door. "What is it, Mrs. Fox?" asked the alarmed neighbor.

"Oh, mercy," cried Mrs. Fox. "My husband is dead! And he has left me without a penny in the world. I suppose now all I can do is throw myself on the mercy of Mr. Toad."

Ha! thought Mr. Fox to himself. She is seeing that villainous old Mr. Toad, it seems. Mr. Fox occasionally worked for Mr. Toad, one of the crime bosses in the old city. He didn't have the backbone to take revenge upon Mr. Toad, but he could certainly teach his wife a lesson.

"All we can do is get the body ready for burial," said Mrs. Fox. "You can help me, Mrs.

Mole." And she fetched a sheet with which to cover the supine Mr. Fox.

Burial, thought Mr. Fox. We'll see about that.

Word spread quickly in the old city, and soon a line was forming outside Mrs. Fox's front door. They weren't creditors—those would come later. They were suitors. A number of seedy characters knew that Mr. Fox had a tidy bit hidden away, and they thought that if they could marry his widow, they might get their hands on his gold.

"Someone here to see you, Mrs. Fox," called Mrs. Mole up the stairs.

"Invite them into the kitchen," called back Mrs. Fox. "I'll be down directly."

Soon the kitchen was full of suitors, and Mrs. Mole poured out coffee and handed round fresh biscuits. One by one, the suitors crept into the living room to have a peak at the deceased Mr. Fox. He looked very dead. But the crafty fox wasn't dead, of course; he was just asleep. His night of carousing had left him more tired than he thought.

Mrs. Mole went up the stairs to check on her friend, and she found the clever Mrs. Fox packed and ready to leave. Tucked into her purse and about her person was Mr. Fox's gold, which he thought he had kept well hidden.

"I'm off to a new life in the new city," Mrs. Fox said to her friend and neighbor. "Take this gold piece and buy yourself and your children something nice."

"Thank you, Mrs. Fox. And bless you." Then Mrs. Mole hurried out of the front door, telling the impatient suitors to wait just another five minutes for Mrs. Fox.

They waited, and they waited. But Mrs. Fox was long gone. She was in a cab on her way to a new life in the new city.

When Mr. Fox suddenly gave a grunting snore, the suitors came piling into the living room and tore away the sheet.

"Why, the scoundrel is alive!" they cried. And they gave Mr. Fox the beating of his life— mostly out of disappointment. It was many days before Mr. Fox was able to be up and about. He had lost his wife, his gold, and whatever pride he had left, and he spent his days and nights complaining about his misfortunes to anyone who would listen. Most didn't.

As for Mrs. Fox, she had enough to set herself up in the new city. Eventually, she opened an orphanage that made its mission the rescue of parentless children from the old city. Mrs. Fox taught her children how to read and write and how to behave, and she sent them out into the wide world to do some good. "For the world," she was often heard to say, "doesn't need any more like my old reprobate of a husband."

## The Elves, or What to Do When You Get an Invitation from the Fairies

Once upon a time in the old city lived a young girl, who was serving maid to a family. The family wasn't exactly poor, but the serving maid had nothing. Her name was Elsa, and she slept in a little garret at the top of the house. The family was miserly and secretive, and they didn't like Elsa much, but they kept her anyway. Even in the old city, having a servant girl was a sign of wealth.

One day, Elsa was sweeping the floor, and she spied a letter sitting in the hearth. Elsa couldn't read, so she took the letter to her mistress, who received it rather suspiciously.

"Why," said her mistress, sweetly, "it's an invitation to attend the Queen of the Fairies on the christening of her child."

Elsa's mistress was no fool, and she watched Elsa expectantly. It was a fine thing to have a serving maid, but Elsa insisted on being fed—and so often. This was her chance to get rid of the girl.

But Elsa was no fool, either—even if she couldn't read. She knew the fairies were trouble. They lived in the suburbs of the old city, and they were constantly stealing children or trying to lure people into their mounds.

But anything is better than this drudgery, thought Elsa. And she got her heavy coat, and she left the house in search of the mound of the Fairy Queen.

It wasn't long before Elsa was met by three fairies, all dressed in jeans and black leather jackets. One had spiked blue hair, the second had a pink Mohawk, and the third was a skinhead. Tough-looking characters.

They led Elsa to the suburbs of the old city, where the roads were split and crumbling, and the houses were falling apart or entirely collapsed. They brought Elsa to what seemed the most ruinous of all the houses, but inside, weirdly enough, was a wide hall, hung with tapestries of gold, and at the far end the Fairy Queen herself, a beautiful lady, wearing rich robes of silver and green, and holding in her arms a fairy baby.

"Welcome, Elsa," said the Fairy Queen with a dazzling smile. "Let the ceremony begin."

Things got underway while Elsa held the baby. The fairies didn't look so scary in their own hall, and after the christening, Elsa laughed and danced and ate to her heart's content. The fairies certainly knew how to have fun.

After what she thought was three days, Elsa told the fairies, "It's time for me to go—back to my life in the old city."

The Fairy Queen filled Elsa's pockets with gold and sent her on her way. The same three fairies guided Elsa back to the old city, but Elsa had a bad feeling. She didn't like the way the one with the pink Mohawk was smirking at her.

She got back to her mistress's front door, but when she turned to thank the fairies, they were gone. Sighing a little, Elsa went into the house. She caught up the broom and began to sweep.

"Where did that chair come from?" she said to herself as she swept. "And I certainly don't remember that at all," she said, looking at a dark-wood bureau, stacked with elegant china dishes and plates.

"What are you doing in my house?" cried a voice behind her.

Elsa whirled to see a woman standing in the kitchen door. She was definitely not Elsa's mistress.

And then she knew. She hadn't been three days with the fairies; it could have been years. "What's the date?" asked Elsa.

The woman was so taken aback by the question, she answered at once.

"Oh, dear," said Elsa. "Seven years, for sure."

Elsa explained to the woman what had happened—how she had gone to visit the fairies on account of the letter. It turned out that Elsa's old master and mistress had died in the meantime, which Elsa found she couldn't be too sad about.

"But you can come and work for me," said the woman, looking Elsa up and down.

Elsa remembered the days of drudgery, and she thought of the gold in her pocket that the fairies had given her. "You know," said Elsa, "I think I'm good."

Elsa left the house, and she set up on her own, not in the old city, but in the new town. She bought a condo overlooking the river, and she went to school. "Reading and writing could come in handy," she said to herself. She didn't stop there. She went on to university courses and got a degree. Then she set up her own consulting business, and she specialized in advising people who received letters from the fairies. She lived very happily, but Elsa could never bring herself to hire a maid.

## Mr. Wolf and the Seven
## Kids, an Urban Fairy Tale

In the twisted heart of the old city lived Mrs. Goat with her seven children. She had to work hard to care for those children. Mr. Goat, who was a drinker and a layabout, had walked out several years before, leaving Mrs. Goat to raise the children on her own. She hadn't been too sorry to see him go.

Being a single parent meant long days and short nights. Mrs. Goat worked two and sometimes three jobs to keep her children in barely more than rags. But they were good children, if not always well behaved, and Mrs. Goat wasn't above giving any of them a clip on the ear to remind them that growing up in the old city didn't mean they could behave like savages.

There weren't many schools in the old city in those days, so the elder children taught the younger to read and write. Mrs. Goat left every morning by seven o'clock. The children usually finished their chores around the house by noon, and that left them the rest of the afternoon and evening to play and snooze and get up to mischief of one kind and another before Mrs. Goat came home again in the early evening.

Every morning, before leaving the house, Mrs. Goat said to the four eldest, twin girls and twin boys—in that order:

"Now, children, finish your chores before doing anything else. Lock the door if you go out for a walk, and never, never, never let a stranger into the house."

"Yes, Mother," the children always said. They did their chores, sometimes they went into the narrow streets to walk or to play, but once back indoors, they never, never, never let anyone into the house.

Now at that time, there were many seedy and unsavory characters living in the old city. One of the worst was Mr. Wolf. He was a tall, thin character, with a mane of gray hair and clean-shaven chops that were an attempt to hide his wolfish disposition. He lived on the main floor of an old warehouse near the river, and he spent his time prowling the streets and looking for victims. He preyed on the weak, the stupid, and the young. So despicable was Mr. Wolf that even the hardest of the hardened criminals gave him a wide berth. Rumors of Mr. Wolf and his exploits were whispered in the dens and taverns of the old city.

"You don't want to mess with the old Wolf," said Mr. Fox, nodding wisely to his companions over mugs of gin-punch. They all shuddered and shook their heads.

The children had heard of Mr. Wolf, but they felt safe enough during the day while their mother was at work—as long as they followed her instructions. "Never, never, never open the door to a stranger," they reminded one another.

One afternoon, while Mrs. Goat was at work, and after the children had finished their chores for the day, they heard a knock at the door. They stopped what they were doing and stared at each other.

"Who could that be?" they whispered to one another.

The eldest set of twins hurried to the door and peeped through the peephole. There, standing on the doorstep, as bold as you please, stood Mr. Wolf.

Mr. Wolf had put on a clean suit that morning. He shaved his long chops carefully, and he brushed back his shaggy hair. He had decided the night before that it was time to make a move to collect Mrs. Goat's children. He had seen them often enough, but they hadn't seen him—he made certain of that. He got to know their habits, morning and afternoon, and today was the day he was going to collect himself some tender and juicy kids.

"Hello, children," called Mr. Wolf, in what he thought was a friendly voice. "I'm the local inspector of schools, and I've come to see that you're educated." He snickered to himself. He thought it was a particularly good joke.

In proof of his lie, he held up a card to the peephole. It read as follows:

Mr. Tobias Wulf
Inspector of Schools.

But the children weren't that stupid. And the golden rule was to never, never, never let a stranger into the house.

"You'll have to come back when our mother is home," called the eldest of the twin girls. "We're not allowed to let a stranger of any kind enter the house."

The twin boys nodded their agreement as they watched their sisters.

Mr. Wolf was a patient sort of predator, but this was too much. Glancing first up and down the street, he drew back his fist, and he hit that door, which burst open with a crash.

There was screaming and running about as the elder children tried to protect the younger. But Mr. Wolf was intent on his business, and all the screaming only served to enrage him further. In no time at all, he had those children trussed up like spring pigs, and two by two he carried them out to his blacked-out van and tossed them inside. He drove away, licking his chops in anticipation, while the children wept and moaned in the back of the van. All, save one.

In his haste to make off with the children, Mr. Wolf had neglected to count his captives. Everyone in that part of the old city knew Mrs. Goat had seven kids, but only six bundles of misery lay on the smelly floor of the van.

The seventh, and youngest, acting on the orders of the eldest twin, had hidden herself in a cupboard while Mr. Wolf tied up the others. She trembled from head to foot, but never a sound did she make as she crouched in the darkness of the cupboard. She felt sorry for her six siblings, but she felt worse at the thought of her mother's return, and having to tell her the tale of the wicked, wicked Mr. Wolf.

Mrs. Goat arrived home as the narrow streets were darkening toward evening. She stepped briskly along, and she knew something was wrong long before she saw the smashed front door. She ran the last half block.

Mrs. Goat stared around at the chaos of the little room. The meager furniture lay scattered about, and in the center of the room was a rabbit stuffy—Fluffy, who belonged to the second youngest. Mrs. Goat paced carefully into the room, one hand sliding into her bag to grasp something out of sight.

With the keen hearing of her kind, she thought she heard a snuffle. She stepped quickly into the kitchen, and she saw that one of the cupboards was not quite shut. Mrs. Goat reached for the cupboard door, opening it to find her youngest, curled up and miserable.

Tragedy had struck the Goat family, but Mrs. Goat did not lose her head. She pulled her youngest daughter out from the cupboard, and the two of them sat at the table, where Mrs. Goat heard the whole, sorry tale.

"And I hid," said her youngest, sniffing back more tears. "I didn't know what to do, (sniff) and I couldn't help the others."

"Don't worry, my dear," said Mrs. Goat, gently rocking her little girl. "You did the right thing. For how would I know that your brothers and sisters had been taken by the terrible Mr. Wolf unless you were here to tell me?"

The little girl nodded sorrowfully. "But what now?" she asked. "Will he eat them?"

"Not if I can help it," said Mrs. Goat determinedly. "Now, come. Get your coat and shoes. We have things to do."

And the two of them set off into the darkness of the streets, all the while with Mrs. Goat clutching something inside her bag.

They walked for a time, but Mrs. Goat knew who she was looking for, and it wasn't long before they found him—slouching and indolent and leaning against a pole.

"Mr. Fox," said Mrs. Goat, marching directly up to him. "I'm interested in seeing your boss."

Mr. Fox shifted on his pole. His expression never changed—if anything, he looked even more indolent and a little scornful. "What makes you think, missus, that I would take you to see the boss?"

Mr. Fox knew exactly who Mrs. Goat was, and he knew of the events earlier that day, but he wasn't about to make things easy for her.

"Because," said Mrs. Goat, "I have a proposition for him. It is to his advantage, and I'm sure you would not want to be the lackey who got in the way of an opportunity for his boss."

Mr. Fox eyed her for a moment. She had spirit, he couldn't deny that. "All right, missus. You come with me. But if the boss isn't happy about being interrupted, then you might regret it."

He led Mrs. Goat down the street and into an alley. They came to a dark doorway, and Mr. Fox gave a secret knock. The door opened. "Follow me, missus. And don't go snooping once we're inside."

Mrs. Goat followed, one hand clutching her daughter, and the other still thrust into her purse. Mr. Fox led them upstairs and down a hall to a door. On the door was a plaque, which read:

Mr. Toad, Crime Boss.

Mr. Fox gave a knock, which was answered by a croaking cough. Mr. Fox gave Mrs. Goat a sly grin. "After you, missus," he said.

Mrs. Goat stepped into the office, her little girl now clutched to her side. It was a small, dingy room, with a desk in the exact middle. A single bare bulb hung from the ceiling by a wire. Behind the desk sat Mr. Toad, leaning back in a chair. The desk before him was littered with takeout containers.

He looked at her out of wide-set, bulging eyes. "Mrs. Goat," said Mr. Toad in a croaking voice. "And what can I do for you this fine evening?"

"I'm here to trade for some information," she said.

"Information?" said Mr. Toad, raising an eyebrow.

"Yes. Mr. Wolf came to my house this afternoon and made off with all my children, save the youngest. If you can please tell me where he hides, then I will agree to come and clean your house twice a week."

Mr. Toad pursed his wide mouth. "Are you suggesting, Madame, that my home requires cleaning?"

"Every man's home requires cleaning," said Mrs. Goat. "And," she said, glancing down at the desk, "I'll bring a home-cooked meal each time I come."

Mr. Toad gulped visibly. Then he blinked. "Done," he said. "Mr. Fox here will take you to the lair of Mr. Wolf, but I don't hold out a lot of hope that you will be able to fulfill your end of the bargain."

"Be that as it may," said Mrs. Goat. "I intend to pay Mr. Wolf a visit."

She followed the slouching Mr. Fox out of the building, and he led her to an old, battered car in the alley. He said nothing as he drove through the narrow streets down to the river. Parking the car in front of an old warehouse, he looked at Mrs. Goat and her child. "I'll wait here awhile," he said. "You have fifteen minutes, and then you're on your own."

Mrs. Goat stepped smartly out of the car. She gathered herself, looked down at her daughter, and then the two of them marched up to the door. It wasn't locked, for who in their right mind would come barging into the lair of Mr. Wolf?

It was a wide room, and Mrs. Goat spotted her children at once—all six of them, trussed up and hanging from hooks in the ceiling. Mr. Wolf stood at a table, chopping onions and mushrooms and wearing a chef's apron. He looked up as Mrs. Goat entered, grinning widely in his long face.

"Well, well," he said. "It looks as though Mrs. Goat has decided to bring me another tasty treat."

Mrs. Goat marched up to the table and stared Mr. Wolf in the eye. "You will release my children right now," she said, the smallest of quivers entering her voice.

But Mr. Wolf smiled even wider, showing his sharp, sharp teeth. "Not likely, Madame. I am here preparing for a night of feasting and excess. And I think my evening just became more excessive."

He was wiping the long chopping knife against his apron to clean it, looking hungrily at the child Mrs. Goat still clutched to her side.

"Very well," said Mrs. Goat, and she took a pistol from her bag and shot him through the heart.

The expression of surprise on old Mr. Wolf's face was something to see. And then he fell over dead on the floor.

Mrs. Goat soon had her six weeping children untied and down from the hooks. Even the littlest helped. And much to the consternation of Mr. Fox, fifteen minutes after he saw Mrs. Goat enter the building, out she came leading a pack of kids.

"I would be very grateful if you drove me and my children home," she said. And Mr. Fox did, but not until after he'd had a quick look inside the warehouse so he could report to his boss.

That night, there was much cause for celebration in the Goat home. Mrs. Goat fixed the door, and her children set to work tidying the living room and preparing a snack.

Mrs. Goat hugged each one of them a hundred times. And she even cried a little, now that all the excitement was over.

"And what lesson can we learn from today's events?" asked Mrs. Goat as her children sat around on the floor eating their snack.

"Don't trust a wolf?" said the eldest.

"It's true," said Mrs. Goat.

"Never, never, never let a stranger into the house—especially a wolf?" said the second youngest, clutching Fluffy.

"True as well," said Mrs. Goat. "But what's also true is that sometimes you just have to take things into your own hands."

After that, things got back to normal in the Goat home. The children were wiser and more cautious, and Mrs. Goat went back to her two and sometimes three jobs. She made good on her promise, and twice a week she tidied the home of Mr. Toad, always leaving a covered platter on his table.

Mr. Toad was perhaps the happiest of all, for he had two home-cooked meals to anticipate every week. And after hearing the story of how Mrs. Goat handled herself in the lair of Mr. Wolf, he decided that he would eventually have to put her on the payroll.

# The Enchanted Pig, a Retelling

From *The Red Fairy Book*, edited by Andrew Lang

Once upon a time there lived a king who had three daughters. One day, the king had to go to war, so he called his daughters and said to them:

"My dear daughters, I must go to war. The enemy is at hand with a terrible army. It is a grief to me to leave you. While I am gone, take care of yourselves, and be good girls. Look after everything in the house. You may walk in the garden, and you may go into all the rooms in the palace, except the room at the end of the hall on the second floor. Into that room you must not enter, for much harm would befall you."

"Don't worry, Father," they replied with dignity. "We would never disobey you. Go in peace, and may you win a glorious victory!"

Upon his departure, the king gave his daughters the keys to all the rooms in the palace. He reminded them once more of the room they mustn't enter. But the parting was hard, and with tears in their eyes, the three daughters hugged their father. "Come back to us!" they cried.

"I will," said the king, gravely. And he hugged his daughters in turn. And with that, he rode from the palace, sitting tall upon his great, black horse.

After that, the three daughters felt so sad and dull that they did not know what to do. To pass the time, and to keep themselves from worrying about their father, they decided they would divide their days between working, reading, and enjoying the garden. All went well for a time, but every day they grew more and more curious about the forbidden room.

"Sisters," said the eldest princess, one afternoon, as they walked through the palace, "all day long we sew, spin, and read. We have explored every corner of the garden, and we have looked into every room in the palace. It is dreadfully dull. Could it hurt to just have a peek in the room at the end of the hall on the second floor?"

"Sister!" cried the youngest. "How can you tempt us to disobey our father? He must have had a good reason for telling us not to go in there. Don't you think?"

"I'm sure," offered the second princess, looking superior, "that the sky won't fall if we just have a peek. It's unlikely dragons and monsters will be lying in wait."

"And how," added the eldest, "will our father ever find out?"

While they talked, they suddenly found themselves in front of the door at the end of the hall on the second floor. With a mischievous smile, the eldest fitted the key into the lock, and snap! The door stood open. With a little shiver of anticipation, one by one, they entered the room.

"Why, it's just an old book," said the eldest, sounding disappointed.

The room was indeed empty, but in the middle stood a large table, with a gorgeous cloth, and on the table lay a big, open book. Still determined to find something interesting, the eldest stepped up to the book and read:

"The eldest daughter of this king will marry a prince from the East."

The eldest gave a little gasp, and then the second princess stepped forward. She turned over the page and read:

"The second daughter of this king will marry a prince from the West."

The sisters were delighted, and they laughed and teased each other. "So, here are some secrets our father is keeping," they said.

The youngest did not want to go anywhere near that book. She hung back, but her sisters dragged her forward. "Turn the page," they said. "Turn the page."

Fearfully, the youngest turned over the page and read:

"The youngest daughter of this king will be married to a pig from the North."

Now, if she had been nearly struck by lightning, the youngest princess would not have been more frightened. She almost fainted from misery, and if her sisters had not held her up, she would have dropped to the floor right there. Once she recovered herself a little, her sisters tried to comfort her, saying:

"How can you believe such nonsense?" said the eldest. "When did it ever happen that a king's daughter married a pig?"

"What a baby you are!" said the second sister. "Won't our father and all his soldiers protect you, even if such a creature came a-wooing?"

The youngest princess felt a little better, but her heart was heavy. She kept thinking about the book and what it said: that happiness awaited her sisters, while she was fated to marry a pig.

Even more, she felt guilty for having disobeyed her father. She grew ill, and in a few days she had gone from being rosy cheeked and merry faced to pale and sickly. She stopped playing with her sisters in the garden, ceased gathering flowers to put in her hair, and never sang as was her wont.

In the meantime, the king had royally trounced the enemy, and he hurried home to his daughters. Everyone went out to meet him before the great gates, and all the people rejoiced at his victorious return. The king went straight into the palace, not even bothering to change out of his dusty cloak and muddy boots.

The three princesses came forward to meet him. His joy was great as he embraced them all in his arms, for he had missed his daughters terribly

It wasn't long before the king noticed that his youngest child was looking thin and sad, and suddenly he felt as if a hot iron were entering his soul, for it flashed through his mind that she had disobeyed him. He felt sure he was right, but to be certain he sat them down and looked at them gravely. "My daughters," he said. "Did you disobey me about the room at the end of the hall on the second floor?"

The three princesses looked at him, and then they burst into tears. "We did, Father! We did!" they cried. "We are dreadfully sorry."

The king was so distressed that he was almost overcome with grief. But he took heart and tried to comfort his daughters, who continued to sob.

"My daughters," he said, gently. "What's done is done, and no amount of tears will change it."

Life slowly got back to normal in the palace, and soon even the youngest forgot about the book and what lay in wait for her.

One fine day, a dashing prince from the East appeared at the court and asked the king for the hand of his eldest daughter. Remembering the words of the book, the king gladly gave his consent. A great wedding banquet was prepared, and after three days of feasting, the happy pair were accompanied to the border with much ceremony and rejoicing. After a month, the same thing befell the second daughter, who was wooed and won by a debonair prince from the West.

Now, when the young princess saw that everything happened exactly as the book had said, she grew sad. She barely ate, and she wouldn't put on her fine clothes nor go out walking, and she declared that she would rather die than marry a pig.

The king tried to comfort his daughter the best he could. "Perhaps things will not come to pass in the manner the book suggests," he said.

But he didn't believe it, and neither did the princess. And despite feeling anxious about what was to come, the princess couldn't help sometimes walking the battlements, watching the north road to see what fate would bring her.

Time passed for the princess, until one fine day an enormous pig from the North walked suddenly into the palace, and going straight up to the king said, "Hail! Oh, King. May your life be as prosperous and bright as sunrise on a clear day!"

"Greetings, friend," answered the king cautiously, "what wind has brought you hither?"

"I come a-wooing," replied the pig.

The king was astonished to hear such a speech from a pig, and he was certain something strange was afoot. He remembered the book and his daughter's fate, but he still didn't want to give the princess in marriage to a pig. As he hesitated, one of the courtiers whispered in his ear that the court and the street were filled with hundreds of pigs. The king saw there was no escape, and he knew he must give his consent. The pig insisted that the wedding should take place within a week, and he refused to go away until the king had sworn a royal oath upon it. What was the king to do?

The king then sent for his daughter. "Your fate is upon you, my dear," he said.

The princess began to weep, but the king said: "My child, the words and demeanor of this pig are unlike any creature I have ever seen. Depend upon it. Some magic is at work. Go with him and obey him. I feel sure that fate has more in store for you than marriage to a pig."

"If you wish me to marry him, dear Father, I will do it," replied the girl, swallowing her tears.

The wedding day arrived, and soon after, the pig and his bride set out for his home in one of the royal carriages. The parting from her father was grievous, but the princess did her best to be brave.

On the road into the North they passed a great bog, and the pig ordered the carriage to stop. He got out and rolled about in the muck until he was covered from head to foot. Then he clambered back into the carriage and turned to his bride. "Kiss me, my dear," he said.

What was the poor girl to do? She remembered her father's words, and, pulling out her pocket handkerchief, she gently wiped the pig's snout and gave it a kiss.

By the time they reached the pig's home, which stood alone in a thick wood, it was dark. They sat down quietly for a little while, as they were tired after their journey. Then they had supper together and lay down to rest. During the night, the princess noticed a strange thing: the pig had changed into a beautiful young man. She was surprised and a little frightened, but remembering her father's words, she took courage. She decided to wait and see what would happen.

Every night after that, she saw that the pig turned into the beautiful young man, and every morning he was back to being a pig. This happened night after night, and the princess knew that her husband must be under an enchantment. As the days passed, she grew quite fond of him, for he was kind and gentle.

One day, as the princess was sitting alone and watching the forest, she saw an old woman walking through the trees. She could hardly contain her excitement, as it was so long since she had seen another human being.

She called out to the old woman: "Come sit with me, old mother. You can join me in a cup of tea."

The old woman joined her, and the two of them were soon deep in conversation. Among many other things, the old woman told the princess that she understood all manner of magic arts, and that she could foretell the future, and she knew the healing powers of herbs and plants.

"I shall be forever grateful, old mother," said the princess, "if you will tell me what is the matter with my husband. Why is he a pig by day and a man by night?"

"I was just going to tell you that very thing, my dear, just to show you what a good fortune-teller I am. He's under an enchantment, of course. If you like, I will give you a charm to break the spell."

"If you only will," sighed the princess. "I will give you anything in return, for I cannot bear to see my poor husband like this."

"Here, then, my dear child," said the old woman, with a curious gleam in her eye. "Take this thread, but don't say anything to your husband, for if you did, it would lose its healing power. Once he is asleep, get up very quietly, and fasten the thread round his left foot. In the morning, you will see no pig beside you, but the beautiful young man.

"And I need no reward. I shall be repaid by knowing that you are happy, for it breaks my heart to think of all you have suffered, and I only wish I had known it sooner, as I should have come to your rescue at once."

After the old woman had gone away into the forest, the princess hid the thread very carefully. That night, she got up quietly, and with a beating heart she bound the thread round her husband's foot. Just as she was pulling it tight, the thread broke with a crack, for it was rotten to the core.

Her husband awoke with a start. He looked at her in the moonlight that streamed through the open window. "Unhappy woman!" he cried. "What have you done? Three more days and this cursed spell would have fallen from me. Now, who knows how long I may have to go about in the shape of a pig?

"I am leaving you at once, and we shall never meet again: not until you have worn out three pairs of iron shoes and blunted a steel staff in your search for me." And so saying, he fled the house and disappeared into the forest.

Finding herself alone, the princess wept so that she thought her heart would break. But after a while, she got up, determined to go wherever fate should lead. On reaching a town, the first thing she did was to buy three pairs of iron sandals and a steel staff, and then she set out in search of her husband.

She wandered over the land, across wide plains and through dark forests. She stumbled over fallen branches, the boughs of the trees striking her face and the shrubs tearing her hands, but on she went, and she never looked back. At last, wearied with her long journey and overcome with sorrow, but still with hope in her heart, she reached a house.

It was the house of the moon. The princess knocked at the door and begged to be let in that she might rest a little. The mother of the moon, seeing the princess's torn clothes and sorrowful face, felt a great pity for her, and she took her in and nursed and tended her. While the princess recovered in the house of the moon, she had a little baby.

"How was it possible for you, a mortal, to come all this way to the house of the moon?" asked the mother of the moon, one day, as the princess sat nursing her child.

The princess told her sad tale. "I shall always be thankful for your kindness to me and my child," the princess concluded, "but I would beg one last favor. Can your daughter, the moon, tell me where I may find my husband?"

"She cannot tell you that, my child," replied the mother of the moon gravely, "but, if you travel toward the east until you reach the house of the sun, you may discover something of your husband." Then she gave the princess a roasted chicken for the journey, and she warned her to be careful not to lose any of the bones.

When the princess had thanked her once more for her care and good advice, and had thrown away one pair of worn-out iron shoes and had put on a second pair, she tied up the chicken into a bundle, and, taking her child in her arms and her staff in her hand, she set out once more on her wanderings.

On and on she went. She crossed wide deserts and scaled high mountains, always walking to the east. The sun burned her face, and the bitter snow of the mountains froze her hands, but on and on she went. At length, wearied to death, her body torn and bleeding, she reached the house of the sun.

With the little strength she had left, the princess knocked. The mother of the sun opened the door and was astonished to find a ragged mortal and her child. She wept with pity upon hearing of all the princess had suffered. "I will do what I can for you, my dear," said the mother of the sun, "but I must hide you in the cellar before my son returns. He is always in a terrible temper at the end of the day."

The mother of the sun helped the princess and her child into a bath, and then she fed them a wholesome supper. After that, she put the princess and her child into the cellar, where she had set up a soft bed. As the weary princess fell asleep, she could hear the sun raging and storming upon his return.

The next day, the princess feared that things would not go well with her. Before leaving the house, the sun grumbled to his mother: "Why does the whole place stink of mortal?"

"The smell of the mortal world can reach us even here, my dear," said his mother, soothingly. "Now, off you go." And the sun stumped off to shine on the world for another day.

"Why is the sun so angry?" asked the princess, later that day. "He is so beautiful and so good to the mortal world."

"Well," said the mother of the sun, "he begins well enough, but watching the wickedness of the world for an entire day puts him in a bad mood.

"Now, I asked my son about your husband, but even he has seen nothing of him. I think your best hope is to journey on to the house of the wind. There you might get word."

When the princess had recovered herself, the mother of the sun gave her a roasted chicken for the journey, and she told her to take care of the bones, for she might have a use for them. The princess then threw away her second pair of iron shoes, which were quite worn out, and with her child on her back and her staff in her hand, she set forth on her way to the wind.

The princess met with even greater difficulties on her way to the house of the wind. She crossed mountains that belched fire and smoke into the sky, entered forests where no mortal foot had trodden, and crossed fields of ice and avalanches of snow.

The poor princess nearly died of these hardships, but she kept a brave heart, and at length she reached an enormous cave in the side of a mountain. It was the house of the wind. The mother of the wind took pity on her and brought the princess and her child inside to give her food and heal her many hurts.

The next morning, the mother of the wind came to the princess, where she had hidden her in the cellar and away from her son. "Your husband, it seems, is living in a thick wood far from here. He has built himself a house from the trunks of trees, where he lives alone, shunning all human companionship."

After the mother of the wind had given the princess a chicken to eat, and had warned her to take care of the bones, she told her to go by the Milky Way, which at night lies across the sky, and to wander on until she reached her goal.

Thanking the old woman and with tears in her eyes, the princess set out on her journey and rested neither night nor day, so great was her longing to see her husband. On and on she walked until her last pair of iron shoes fell to pieces. She threw them away and went on in bare feet, not heeding the thorns that wounded her, nor the stones that bruised her. At last, she reached the edge of a dark wood. With her child on her back, she slashed her way into the wood with her steel staff, until it was quite blunt. She threw it away, overcome with despair.

It was then, in a little clearing, that she noticed a house made of the trunks of trees. It had no window, and the door was in the roof. What was she to do? How was she to get in?

Then, she thought of the chicken bones that she had carried all that weary way, and she said to herself: They would not all have told me to take such good care of these bones if they had not had some good reason for doing so. Perhaps now, in my hour of need, they may be of use to me.

She took the bones out of her bundle, and having thought for a moment, she placed the two ends together. To her surprise, they stuck tight. Then she added the other bones, until she had two long poles the height of the house. Across them she placed the other bones, piece by piece, like the steps of a ladder. As soon as one step was finished, she stood upon it and made the next one, and then the next, till she reached the door in the roof. With her child on her arm, she entered the door of the house. Here she found everything in perfect order. Having taken some food, she sat down with her child to rest.

When her husband, the pig, came back to his house, he was startled by what he saw. At first he could not believe his eyes, and he stared at the ladder of bones. He felt that some fresh magic must be at work, and in his fear he almost turned away from the house. But then, he changed himself into a dove, so that no witchcraft could have power over him, and he flew into the room without touching the ladder. Here he found his wife rocking a child. At the sight of her, looking so changed by all that she had suffered for his sake, his heart was moved by such love and longing and by so great a pity that the enchantment that was upon him broke, and he became a man.

The princess stood up when she saw him, and her heart beat with fear, for she did not at first know him. But suddenly she recognized her husband, and in her great joy she forgot all her sufferings, and they lifted from her like a cloak. He was a very handsome man, as straight as a fir tree. They sat down together and she told him all her adventures, and he wept with pity at the tale. And then he told her his own history.

"I am a king's son," he told her. "Once, my father was fighting against a family of dragons, who were the scourge of our country. I slew the youngest dragon myself. His mother, who was also a witch, cast a spell over me and changed me into a pig. It was she who, in the disguise of an old woman, gave you the thread to bind round my foot. So that, instead of the three days that had to run before the spell was broken, I was forced to remain a pig for three more years. Now that we have suffered for each other, and have found each other again, let us forget the past."

And in their joy, they kissed one another. The next morning, they set out early to return to his father's kingdom. Great was the rejoicing of all the people when they saw the prince and his princess and their child. His father and mother embraced them both, and there was feasting in the palace for three days and three nights.

Then they set out to see the father of the princess. The old king nearly went out of his mind with joy at beholding his daughter again. When she had told him all her adventures, he said to her:

"Did not I tell you that I was quite sure that that creature who wooed and won you as his wife had not been born a pig? Great has been your suffering, my child, but greater has been your courage, and rich will be your reward."

And as the king was old, he put them on the throne in his place. And they ruled as only kings and queens rule who have suffered many things. And if they are not dead, they are still living and ruling happily.

# The Dream of the Tree

Once there was a man who had a dream that ruined his life. In the dream, he was walking across a vast country. He was not just walking—he was *striding*. He was striding with seven-league steps so that the ground beneath him and about him blurred and shimmered. He passed through forests, over great plains of grass, and through the gaps between mountains. He strode on until he saw a mountain rising up before him. It was a mountain as he had never seen a mountain before. It went up and up, climbing higher and higher until it was lost in the sky.

He paused at the foot of the mountain and looked up. There was only one thing to do. He began to climb.

He went up and up, stepping over streams, across wide meadows, and over stands of trees. He went on until he came to the end of the trees, where there was only rock. He kept climbing.

This mountain, he thought, was surely the highest mountain in the world. He climbed and climbed.

Finally, after what seemed a year and a day, the man arrived at the top of the mountain. Across a great plain, the man could see a tree. It was surely the tallest tree he had ever imagined. It went up and up until, impossibly far overhead, the tree spread its branches.

The man walked across the plain toward the foot of the immense tree. As he did, his seven-league strides kicked up swirls of leaves. There were countless numbers of them, and as he caught one of the leaves, he realized that each leaf held a story, or a fragment of a story.

He caught leaf after leaf. He read snatches of stories about people who lived and died and who fought tremendous battles. He read stories of boys and girls, stories of men and women who wandered far, searching for love, for revenge, and for treasure. He read snatches of stories about patience and greed and the longing that goes with lost love, friendship, and family.

The man looked up to the great tree. "This must be the tree where all stories come from," he said aloud to himself.

He hurried forward to the trunk of the massive tree that rose up like a wall before him. Reaching out a hand, he touched the trunk of the great tree. For one, indefinable moment, he had a glimpse of the ongoing story of the world, from its beginning in the depths of space and time to its conclusion at the end of all things…

And then he woke. The cry that escaped his lips in that moment was a cry of grief and loss. The man had glimpsed for one instant the story of the world, and as he sobbed aloud in the gray morning, the dream began to fade.

Later that day, the man sold his house and everything he owned. He took the money from the sale of all of his belongings, and he wrapped it in a handkerchief with a loaf of bread. He left the home where he had lived all of his life and took to the road. He told himself that he was going to find that tree, even if he had to search to the ends of the earth, for he wanted just one more glimpse into that story.

And so he did. He wandered far and met many people, and to whomever would listen, he would tell what he could remember of that story and the fragments he read on the leaves. Many people thought him mad, and others just thought him a storyteller. Some were glad of his stories, but many were not, for in everyone he met, he planted a seed of that longing for the story he glimpsed when he touched the tree in his dream.

# The Story of Nell,
# a Fairy Tale

# 1

Once upon a time there lived a young girl with her father. Her name was Nelly, or Nell for short. She worked hard to keep the house in order and do what she could for her father. He was a good man, and he was lame.

Nell's father was a woodcutter. One day, while cutting down a tree, he was distracted by a voice as the tree fell, and he was struck by a branch and pinned to the ground. He lay there all night, until Nell came looking for him in the morning.

There were just the two of them, for Nell's mother had died many years before. When her father didn't come home from the forest, Nell waited up. She wasn't too worried, because she knew that many things could happen in the

forest. But at dawn, Nell put a cloak over her dress and apron; she put on her heavy shoes, and she went out to look for him.

She eventually found him, and she was able to cut the branch of the tree that was pinning her father to the ground. He was free, and he was alive, but he was badly hurt. She got him back to their little cottage, but after that he was lame in the leg and couldn't work as a wood-cutter anymore.

So, her father became a carver. He was able to work in the garden and help in the house, and he and Nell lived poorly, if happily, for many years. Once a week, they went to the market in the town that was beyond the edge of the forest, and there the woodcutter sold his carvings, and Nell sold her jam and her baking, which was some of the best at the market.

It went on like that until, one day, Nell became restless. "I have never seen the world," she said to her father.

Her father was sitting on the step before the front door, carving a spoon. He looked at her. "If you want to see the world," he said, "then go with my blessing."

But Nell hesitated. "What about you, my father? How will you manage without me?"

The woodcutter, who was now a woodcarver, smiled gently. "I will be fine, my daughter," he said. "There are some in the village who will make sure I am fine. I will carve in the winter and tend the garden in the summer. Although I'm sure those who come to the market will miss your jams and your baking."

Nell thought about it long and hard. "I will go away," she said to her father, after a week. "But I will come back, and when I do, I will know more of the world."

Her father bowed his head. "So be it," he said.

A week later, Nell gathered a few things into a sack she had stitched from an old coat of her mother's; she put on her walking shoes, took up a stick, and off she went at dawn.

# 2

Nell walked until she came to the village. It looked peaceful in the gray light of morning. She said a good-bye in her heart, gripped her stick, and took the high road.

Nell walked and walked all that day, seeing nothing unusual and encountering only one or two other travelers. At sunset, Nell stopped for the night, making herself a camp beneath the trees. She eventually wrapped herself in her cloak and blanket and fell asleep, listening to the whisper of leaves in the darkness.

Nell woke suddenly. She opened her eyes to the glare of torches. There was a hand before her face. It wasn't very clean—the nails were especially dirty—and it was holding a long knife.

"What do we have here?" said a growling voice, as Nell sat up.

She looked around to see a group of men, all bandits, most certainly, and all leering and grinning nasty grins. They were dressed in heavy leather jerkins and breeches and boots. Some carried knives and some carried short clubs.

"You are going to come with us, my pretty," said the one who had held the knife to Nell's face. "And if you behave yourself, we won't kill you right away."

Nell stood up and looked at the bandits. The one who had held the knife to her face seemed to be the leader. "Let me gather my things," she said.

The bandits looked at one another. Weren't girls supposed to scream and cry and carry on? The bandit leader made a horrible face. "Now you're going to come with us, and you're not going to make a sound. Understand, girly?"

Nell nodded. "You may want to put that knife away. You may cut yourself." Nell was aware of how dangerous knives could be.

The bandit leader glared at her. "Just you keep quiet," he said, snarling. "Keep your tongue in your head or I might decide to cut it out."

Nell smiled and nodded once again. The bandits looked again at one another, and this time they grinned.

The bandit leader led the way through the trees until they came to the bandit hideout. They had clearly been out all night, for they started grumbling about supper and who was going to make it.

"Your turn," said one of the bandits, shoving the shoulder of his companion.

"No!" cried another. "Not his turn. He'll poison us all!"

"I'll make you supper," said Nell. And the bandits looked at their leader hopefully.

The leader turned to Nell before the door of the bandit hideout. "Now," he said, with a snarl. "Just you make us something tasty. If you don't, we may have you for supper!"

The others laughed, trying to sound as bandits and dangerous as possible, but it wasn't very convincing, because they were now only thinking of their supper.

Nell set to work. She told the bandits to sit at the table and wait quietly. She frowned at the state of the stove, but soon she had a great pot of stir-about bubbling and steaming. Opening a small pouch at her belt, Nell took a large pinch of herbs from a cloth. Nell knew all about herbs. She added it to the stir-about.

Soon she was doling out the stir-about into bowls, while the bandits waited obediently for their supper. They ate greedily, shoveling in the food and not saying a word, while Nell filled their tankards and bowls. It wasn't long before they were yawning and nodding where they sat, and one by one, they put their shaggy heads onto their arms and fell fast asleep.

Nell sighed, looking at the lot of them around the table. She quickly got her things together. She thought of leaving them a note, but she doubted if any of them could read. She left the hideout and walked briskly through the forest, as the sky began paling toward dawn.

**3**

Nell walked until the sun was up, when suddenly she came upon an animal by the side of the road. It was a great, gray wolf, and it was injured. It stared at her out of great, yellow eyes, and it said in a gravelly voice,

"Come close, my dear, and I will eat you up."

Nell stepped up to the wolf unconcernedly. "I don't believe you will eat me up," she said. "You are injured. You are in no shape to eat anyone up."

The wolf gave a sigh and a whine. "Please help me, young maiden," he whimpered. "If you don't, the woodsman will surely come and cut off my head."

Nell knelt down and peered at the wolf. He had a deep gash along his back leg, but Nell could tell he was mostly weak from lack of food and water. She gave him something to drink, and then she gave him something to eat, and then she tended his wound. The water and food revived the wolf. He sat up and looked at Nell.

"And what," he said, "is a young maiden doing walking the high road alone?"

"I am seeking adventure and seeing the world," said Nell.

"Then you will need a companion and a protector," said the wolf.

Nell thought for a moment. "A companion might be good," she said, looking hard at the wolf.

He bowed his head. "Then I will be your companion."

So the two of them carried on down the high road. They walked and they walked, sometimes stopping to rest. The wolf told Nell all about his life in the forest, of how people were afraid of him, of how the hunters and woodsmen of the forest always tried to kill him.

"Perhaps if you didn't threaten to eat people, they might leave you alone," said Nell reasonably. "You don't have to act like the wolf of the stories, you know."

The wolf thought about that. "It isn't easy," he said. "People are afraid of me no matter what I do. It's just simpler most of the time to be the wolf they expect."

Nell wasn't convinced.

They walked on until they came to a kingdom without a king. It was a wide land of pastures and clumps of woodland, but all seemed abandoned. The wolf told Nell the story of the place. "Once upon a time," he said, "this was a great kingdom. People came from far and wide to visit the court. The floating gardens of the palace were one of the wonders of the northern world, and the king's library held more books than any for a thousand miles."

"It sounds lovely," said Nell.

"Indeed," said the wolf. "But the king was a strange king. He had a way of letting the people govern themselves. The people appointed mayors to govern the towns, and reeves to help govern the boroughs. Every borough sent a representative to the king's council. Very odd," finished the wolf.

"Why odd?" asked Nell.

The wolf looked at her. "You don't know much about kings, do you?"

Nell ignored the remark. "What's happening there now?"

"Well," said the wolf. "The king vanished. Some say he died, and some say he was put under a curse by an evil magician. The prince has taken over, but he's not much of a prince. Too afraid to do anything. He doesn't trust the people, so he mostly hides in the palace and keeps everyone away. The gardens and the library are closed, and the queen grieves for her husband. The king's council no longer meets, and the soldiers run amuck. And worst of all, a dragon has taken to pillaging the kingdom."

"Well," said Nell, "perhaps we should pay a visit."

The wolf bowed his head. "As you wish. I will do my best to protect you and guide you." They walked on.

The sun was high as they came to the borders of the kingdom. The road ran up to a gate, behind which was a fortress. It looked deserted in the afternoon light. The gates hung, burned and twisted, and no guards paced the wall.

"It doesn't look good," commented Nell as they approached the gate. The wolf said nothing. The fortress rose high on either side of the gate, and the road that ran between was lost in shadow.

They were making their way past the broken gates and into the gloom of the road when a shadow split itself away from the wall and ran. With a bound, the wolf was after the shadow, and with a crash and a cry, the wolf had something pinned to the ground. Nell hurried up. It writhed and squealed and squeaked.

"Let me go! Let me go! I ain't done nothin'!"

# 4

The thing on the ground was making such a fuss that it took a moment before Nell could understand what she saw. "Come on," said Nell. "Bring him out into the light."

The wolf picked up the unfortunate squeaker like a sack. He trotted forward to where the road ran out from the shadow of the fortress, and he dropped his burden in a heap.

Nell peered down. Lying before the feet of the wolf was a disheveled young man—hardly more than a boy. "Now, stop your noise," said Nell, sternly. "Who are you, and what has happened here?"

The boy gave a sniff, and he looked up at Nell. "It's the dragon, Miss. It comes a-marauding every night. 'Tis said no man can stand against it. It burns and destroys wherever it goes. It eats the people's cattle and sheep, and it carries off the young folk to its lair. I always thought dragons was particular about maidens, but this one don't care. Carries off all the young folk it can find. It almost got me the other night."

Nell thought it was time to interrupt the boy's story. "What is your name?" she asked kindly.

"It's Norman, Miss. I'm the smith's boy," said Norman with a sniff. He looked askance at the wolf. "Is he going to eat me, then?"

Nell laughed. "No," she said. "This wolf is my friend. He won't hurt you."

"Now, what about the prince?" asked Nell more brusquely. "Is he not doing anything about this monster?"

Norman looked at her out of round eyes. "The prince?" he said, his voice rising again to a squeak. "The prince is mad—or perhaps just terrified, Miss. They say he has closed the palace up to any and all of his people. He is afraid the dragon will come and take his Royal Highness, so he has locked himself away. He won't let any-one near—not even his Royal Mother."

Nell looked thoughtful. She glanced at the wolf. "Perhaps we should pay a visit to the prince," she said.

"He won't let you near," warned Norman. "He's mad, like I say."

"Be that as it may," said Nell. "We are go-ing to go and ask him what he intends to do about this dragon. Having a dragon rampaging over the land simply won't do."

Norman sprang to his feet. "Then I will come with you, Miss!" he cried. He held up two weedy arms. "I may be just a smith's boy, but I'm strong, Miss. If you intend to do some-thing about this terrible dragon, then I want to help."

Nell looked at him skeptically, and then at the wolf. The wolf looked back impassively.

"I can at least show you the way," said Norman hopefully.

Nell didn't bother pointing out that the road would probably lead right to the palace. "Very well," she said. "You may join us."

"I am at your service," said Norman, bowing low.

"You need not be at my service," said Nell. "But you are free to accompany my companion and me for as long as you like."

And with that, the three of them turned and began walking down the road, Norman chattering away about the kingdom, the dragon, and a very special milkmaid he had a fancy for back home.

The way was long, and not until nearly sunset did the companions arrive at the palace. But arrive they did, and it was a sight to behold.

The dragon's marauding feet had crushed and trampled the grass and gardens all around the palace, but, oddly enough, nothing seemed burned or destroyed. The famous floating gardens were hidden by a mist over the lake, and the palace itself was shrouded by a roiling fog. The light was fading, and the air was damp. Nell shuddered in her heavy travelling cloak. The wolf's eyes seemed to glow in the strange light, and Norman's teeth rattled in his head.

"H-h-here w-w-w-we are," stuttered Norman, from cold or fear Nell wasn't sure.

Nell peered through the fog to where she could just see the outline of a broad set of marble steps leading up to the palace doors.

"Any suggestions?" asked Nell.

"I suggest you knock," said the wolf. "This place seems under an enchantment, but I see no harm in trying."

Nell nodded, and she walked across to the broad steps, peering up at the great palace doors. They looked uninviting. But with a quick breath of resolve, Nell mounted the steps, and spotting a knocker in the shape of a dragon's head, she knocked three times, the sound booming and echoing weirdly in the foggy air.

# 5

The echoes had died, and Nell was prepared to knock again, when suddenly she heard the sound of a great bar sliding back. With a rumble and a creak, one of the doors opened a crack.

"Go away!" cried a voice. "Can't you see this place is under a curse?"

"Yes," said Nell, "but we want to help."

"No! No! Now, go away!"

But Nell wasn't about to be put off. She wedged the toe of her heavy shoe into the crack of the door. "Now, listen," she said, patiently. "We want to help. Open this door and let us inside." She looked back down the stairs and waved her companions forward. The wolf leaped up the stairs, while Norman came tripping up behind.

The sound of complaint and protest came from behind the doors, but Nell ignored it. "Come on," she said to Norman, "grab hold."

The two of them seized the edge of the great door and heaved. As the door swung wide, there came a shriek from the darkness inside, and then the sound of running feet.

As Nell caught her balance, the wolf slipped past and into the darkness. A moment later, he had a figure pinned to the floor.

"We need some light," said Nell, and Norman found a lamp and lit it with his flint and tinder. In the soft glow of the light, Nell saw the wolf, one paw holding a figure on the floor.

"Your Highness," gasped Norman.

Nell peered down at what must be the prince. He was a mess. His face and hair were grimed with soot, his clothes spattered with grease and food stains.

"Let me up this instant!" cried the prince, writhing beneath the paw of the wolf.

"Let him up," said Nell, and the wolf released him.

The prince sat up at once. He glared around at them. "Peasants! And a dog," he spluttered contemptuously.

The wolf bristled.

"What do you think you are doing?" asked the prince. "I should have your heads cut off and mounted outside the palace walls."

Nell looked at him levelly. He was hardly more than a boy. "Indeed," she said. "And just who would cut off our heads? Not you, surely?"

The prince scrambled to his feet. Even in the soft light of the lamp, Nell could see his face reddening with fury. "When I find my guard," he said, "I will have them cut off your heads in the courtyard. No, better yet, I'll have you drawn and quartered first. Then I'll have your heads cut off."

The wolf gave a long, low growl, which caused the prince's eyes to nearly pop out of his head. But Nell had had enough.

"You are not going to have anyone beheaded," she said. "You are going to help us deal with the dragon and restore your kingdom."

"I…" cried the prince. "I had nothing to do with it. It was my father, the king, who befriended the wicked old sorcerer, and who brought the dragon upon the kingdom. He's the one who should deal with the dragon. Go talk to him…or go talk to my mother."

Nell looked at the prince for a long time. "You," she said, slowly, "are a disgrace. You do not deserve the name of Prince. You are a selfish brat."

She turned to her companions. "Let's begin a search for the queen," she said. "I'm sure we will get better sense and more help from her."

Norman, who had been in the palace before, led the way. "We will first check the royal bower," he said. And the three companions set off into the darkness, leaving the prince to shriek curses after them.

But the queen was not in the royal bower. They knocked and knocked, the sound echoing down the empty halls.

"Any ideas?" asked Nell.

Norman looked uncertain. "We could look in the gardens," he said, "or maybe the library."

"You will find her in my father's private library," said a voice from farther down the
passage.

Nell looked. It was the prince, who had followed them up from the main hall. His dislike of
them wandering around his palace had clearly
overcome his desire not to do anything. He
had found a cloak and sword. He looked more
prince-like, but no less friendly.

"I will take you to my mother. She will want
to see you." And he stalked away down the
passage.

The three companions looked at one another, then followed the prince. As bad tempered
and ill-mannered as he was, the prince knew
the castle better than they. So off they went,
following the prince, who marched sullenly in
front.

Down corridors and upstairs they went.
Until, at last, the prince pointed to a door
at the top of some stairs. "There," he said.
"Mother has been looking through books
of my father's. Much good it will do her," he
grumbled.

Nell reached for the handle of the door, and they crowded inside.

There, sitting at a long table, was a woman in a comfortable tunic and breeches. She wore high leather boots, and her hair was tied back in a loose bun. She was studying a book that lay before her on the table, looking up as the companions entered. "Well," she said. "Help at last."

"Your Highness," cried Norman, and he threw himself onto one knee. Nell was about to kneel as well.

"Now, now," said the queen. "None of that. We have a dragon to vanquish, and a kingdom to save."

Nell introduced herself and her companions. "We want to help…if we can," she concluded. Nell found herself liking the queen much more than the prince.

"You can, indeed," said the queen. She looked at them thoughtfully. "My husband, the king, was spirited away one year ago by an evil sorcerer. Since that day, a dragon has been ravaging the kingdom. I have looked through all of my husband's books, and it seems such a monster can only be killed using a cursed blade—this blade, in fact."

From the table, the queen picked up a long knife. It was blackened and battered, and it had an ugly look.

Nell peered at the knife uneasily. "That knife will kill the dragon?" she asked.

"Yes," said the queen gravely.

"That will be my task!" cried Norman. "Give me the knife, Your Highness, and I will slay this monster."

Nell looked at the wolf. He rolled his eyes.

"Bravely spoken, good Norman," said the queen. "But I'm afraid the task of piercing the dragon's heart falls to my son."

"What!" shrieked the prince. "I'm not going to stab any dragon, let alone go near the thing. Let the peasant do it. He seems keen enough."

"My son," said the queen, even more gravely. "You are the prince, and this task is for you. But you will not be alone. You have these brave companions to help you."

"They're commoners!" scoffed the prince. "How can they help? And anyway, I don't want to do it."

"But you must." The queen's voice had taken on a steely note. "And, my son, even the greatest of heroes—prince or princess, milkmaid or stable boy—always has help from brave companions."

Nell was getting a bad feeling about all of this. It wasn't just that they had to kill a dragon, or that this brat of a prince didn't seem up to the job. Something else was bothering her. If the dragon had been marauding for a year, why hadn't it burned the castle to the ground by now?—especially considering the monster had been to the castle often enough to despoil the grounds. But Nell didn't have the chance to think it through, for the prince was throwing a royal tantrum.

"I won't! I won't!" He was actually stamping his foot. "Kill the dragon yourselves, but leave me out of it." And with that, the prince turned and raced out of the room.

As she listened to the prince clattering down the stairs, Nell knew with a sinking heart that saving the kingdom was going to be more complicated than she had first thought.

# 6

**N**ell stood at the head of a valley with her companions. After discussing dragon-slaying strategies with the queen, she and the others had taken a short rest, eaten some food, and then got ready to meet the dragon.

The queen looked grave as she bid them farewell. "I am sorry about my son," she said. "I do not ask you to do this," she added, looking at Nell.

"But if your son isn't willing," said Nell, "then someone must try to stop the dragon."

The queen nodded. "I have misgivings about sending you and your companions to fight such a monster."

Nell had misgivings of her own, but she found most of them hard to put into words. "Who is the sorcerer who put the spell on the king? And where is the king?"

"Perhaps the sorcerer is holding my husband captive, but I fear he is no longer alive. As for the sorcerer himself, I'm not sure. My husband told me a story, long ago. He said that he met someone on his travels whom he thought was a sorcerer or a wizard, but he would never talk about it."

And that was all Nell learned. And now, she stood at the top of a valley, looking down into a haze of smoke and steam, carrying a cursed knife, and getting ready to fight a dragon with two companions—a wolf and a boy.

"The dragon lies below," said the wolf.

Norman simply stared, his eyes round. He was clutching a spear, and he was now dressed in a helmet and chain-mail coat, which Nell knew would do nothing at all against the dragon.

"Well," said Nell. "Let's go." And the companions began the long walk into the valley.

As they moved deeper between the hills, the air became thicker, and breathing was difficult. Clouds of smoke and steam drifted past the companions, and Nell wondered how long they could endure this terrible place. The grass and trees were blackened and burned. The ground was churned and broken by the passing of the monster, and here and there were the blackened ruins of what once must have been huts and farmhouses.

The air was heavy—no sound of birds, and no breath of wind. Nell felt the ground rising before her feet. As she and her companions came to the top of the rise, before them, emerging out of the smokes and steams, lying half on its side, with its great head and forelegs facing them, was the dragon.

Even though the monster was lying in a hollow, its head was on a level with the companions. Its body, with its dark, roughened hide, long as a ship, was stretched out behind, its spiked tail disappearing into the reek.

At first, all Nell could notice was the eyes— great, yellow eyes with the vertical pupils of a cat. The eyes looked directly at her, and Nell looked back, mesmerized.

She wasn't sure what she saw in those eyes—something bestial, but something else, submerged beneath the rage and the animal violence. Was it pain, perhaps? Or maybe it was a need or a desire beyond anything she understood.

Nell tore her eyes from those of the dragon, and then she could see that the creature's left hind leg was stretched out at an odd angle. It looked hurt—possibly broken. Nell felt a sudden surge of compassion for this beast. For it was a beast, and it was acting according to its nature, regardless of what that was. The queen had said that she must plunge the cursed knife into the heart of the monster in order to kill it, but Nell wondered if such a thing was even possible.

Holding the eyes of the dragon once again, Nell began to walk slowly down the far side of the rise.

"Be careful, Nell!" cried Norman. "It will probably eat you!" He and the wolf followed close behind Nell, although there was little either of them could do to protect Nell or themselves.

The monster watched Nell's approach, lowering its head as she did so, until its long, horned head and jaw lay flat to the ground between its clawed feet.

Nell did not take her eyes from those of the dragon, and she still held the cursed knife in her left hand. She slowly reached out her right and touched the dragon. Its gray-black hide was hard as stone and hot to the touch. It reminded Nell of the outside wall of the baker's house back in her village.

Nell was beside the head of the monster now, and she held its eye. She thought she saw something else in that eye—a pleading?

Nell looked down to the great foreleg that reached forward, leaving an angle where the hide of the monster looked less like roughened stone. If she plunged the knife right there, she just might strike the creature's heart. Nell clutched the knife and took a breath.

At that moment, the wolf gave a howl and Norman a cry. Nell couldn't see anything beyond the body of the monster, but she guessed well enough. She heard a high-pitched, squeaky cry. The prince had decided to join them.

The monster reared up, and Nell caught a glimpse of the prince, lunging in and stabbing at the dragon with a sword that was far too big for him—the idiot.

No time now to try and reach the monster's heart. Nell stabbed wildly with the cursed knife, catching the beast barely a glancing blow on its iron flank. But the shock of the stab ran up Nell's arm, numbing it to the shoulder and causing her to gasp with pain, while the dragon gave a screeching bellow that sounded like mountains being torn asunder.

Nell staggered as the monster writhed and flailed. She felt herself caught, then dragged away as the air filled with choking smoke and steam. And as the world spun and churned around her, Nell had one thought: her father would have liked to hear this story.

# 7

## The Last Chapter

**N**ell woke slowly. She was lying in a soft bed and looking up at an unfamiliar ceiling. "Where am I?" she said to herself.

She felt a cold nose in her hand, and she looked over to see the gray wolf sitting beside her bed. Gathered around were several people: Norman, his hair singed and round eyes anxious; the queen, her face grave, and still wearing her riding clothes; and the prince, his arm in a sling and a smirk on his face. As for the other person, Nell didn't know him. He was tall, a little stooped, and his dark hair and beard were streaked with gray.

"Hello," said Nell. "What has happened?"

"My lady lives!" cried Norman, a hand to his heart.

Nell tried to sit up, but the queen leaned forward and gently pressed her back into the pillows.

"You must not move too quickly," said the queen. "You have suffered a great shock—not to mention saving both the kingdom and my husband."

Nell looked curiously at the queen. "Your husband?" she asked.

The queen smiled. "Yes, but all in good time."

The man whom Nell did not know made an awkward bow. His leg seemed injured. "Nell," he said. "I am pleased to make your acquaintance. You have saved me, my son, and the kingdom."

Nell was confused, but she still felt tired. "Tell me all about it when I wake up," she said, and went immediately back to sleep.

Nell heard the story of the dragon several times in the next few days. Norman and the prince each had their own versions, but Nell found the king's to be the most interesting.

It appeared that the wicked sorcerer had put a spell on the king. The king himself had become the dragon that had laid waste to most of the kingdom. "But I hadn't entirely lost my sense of who I was," said the king to Nell. "Even as the dragon, I couldn't destroy the gardens or the palace itself. I created those gardens for the queen many years ago. They were," he added, "an anniversary present, don't you know. Some part of me remained human—enough to keep me from destroying everything, and enough to enable me to recognize that you, Nell, had come to set me free. Once you touched me with the cursed blade, the spell was broken. Of course, if you had plunged the knife into my heart, I would have been dead as well."

Nell sighed. "I knew something was odd," she said. "But I still tried to kill you—the dragon, I mean. It was really the prince who saved you. If he hadn't come at you with his sword, I would have stabbed you in the heart."

"Perhaps," said the king, with a gentle smile. "The point is that you broke the spell and saved both me and the kingdom, not to mention your companions. As for my son—he believes himself a hero, so we will let him think so—at least for a while."

"One thing," said Nell. "Why did the sorcerer put the spell on you in the first place? The queen said that you had met a sorcerer years ago. Was it the same one?"

The king paused for a long time. Finally, he sighed. "I did a foolish thing, Nell. I was a young man, and I desired peace for my kingdom above all else. I didn't realize at the time that even wishing for peace, as noble as it seemed at the time, was the vanity of a young man. Peace can only come with the help of others. Only sacrifice can lead to gain. As a young man, I promised the sorcerer that if I could reign in peace, one of my sons would go with him as his prentice.

"Well, the years passed, and I only had one son, and not a very good one at that. The prince tries, but he has much to learn. When the sorcerer came to take my son as his prentice, I refused. The sorcerer was angry, of course, and he cursed me and the kingdom. But you, Nell, have saved us all."

Nell was content to let the king think so, but she felt that things had managed to just work out all right. They could have gone very differently in that valley.

Perhaps the wolf put it best. "Every hero needs his or her companions—just as the queen said. Even the prince had his part to play, but it was your hand that wielded the cursed knife."

Nell wasn't sure if the words of the wolf were helpful or not, but she was content for the time being. After several days, during which the castle was as busy as a hive of bees, Nell went to the queen. "I must return home to my father," she said. "He's probably wondering if I'm even alive."

Nell thought the queen would try to convince her to stay, but she smiled. "You have restored my son's father to him, my husband to me, and the king to his people. Go and find your own father, Nell. But you are welcome in the palace at any time."

The next morning, Nell and the wolf took to the road. Norman didn't come, but Nell could tell he wanted to. "You are needed here," she said. "Stay, serve the king and queen, and help rebuild the kingdom."

Norman nodded, silently, and a single tear trickled down his cheek. Nell hugged him. "We will see one another again," she said. "Don't worry."

Nell and the wolf said their good-byes to the king, the queen, and the prince, and off they went. It was an uneventful journey, but the roads were crowded with people returning to the kingdom. The wolf slipped off the road whenever another group appeared on the road. Nell heard the story of the slaying of the dragon more than once from travelers. Some said the prince had slain the dragon, and others told the story of a great warrior princess from the north, who had come to slay the monster and free the kingdom. And some said that the king, who had been transformed into a dragon, fought the sorcerer in the form of a great wolf, and when the dragon had slain the wolf, the spell had broken. Nell listened to all of the stories and smiled.

At last, Nell and the wolf came back to the edge of her own village. "Here I must leave you," said the wolf. "No one will be happy to see a wolf in the village."

"I suppose," said Nell. "But you will come and visit?"

"Of course," said the wolf, and the great beast licked Nell's hand once and bounded away into the forest.

"Here I am again," said Nell to herself, looking at the empty road. She felt a little sad. But she set off again, passing by the village, and taking the path into the forest that would lead to her home.

It was dusk by the time she came to the cottage in the trees. And there, sitting on the steps as though he had never been anywhere else, sat her father, carving a tall walking stick from a branch of ewe wood.

When he saw Nell, he stood up, his face smiling in the twilight, and tears running down his weathered face. "You have come home, my daughter," he said.

"I have, Father," said Nell, hugging him tightly. "I've been and seen the world. And, I think, it will make for a good story."

"Then you must tell me all about it," said her father. And they went inside the cottage, where the woodcarver put on the kettle for tea, and he sat in his armchair to hear the story of Nell's adventures.

## Afterward

When my daughters were young, we were living in university housing, and we told stories every night at bedtime. One day, I was making dinner, and I started to tell my youngest a story. It was "Goldilocks and the Three Pigs."

That was my first experience of telling a fractured fairy tale. I didn't know the term at the time, but I had taken a course in storytelling from Gail de Vos at the University of Alberta, and she encouraged us to play with stories.

After that, I began to encounter fractured fairy tales, and I have to admit, I didn't like them much. As a storyteller, I thought of myself as something of a purist. I wanted what I thought were the original tales. I read and told Grimms' tales, and I even learned a story from the Welsh Mabinogion, "The Tale of Branwen," which I told at a storytelling festival held at the Rockwood Centre in Sechelt, on the beautiful Sunshine Coast.

My kids grew up, and they didn't want stories at bedtime as much anymore. I learned something about folk and fairy tales, and soon I began teaching them in my children's literature classes.

My first understanding of the interconnectedness of folktales and fairy tales came from reading Joseph Campbell's *A Hero with a Thousand Faces.* I learned about the ways stories speak across culture and across religion, the way they tie back to dreams and dreaming, and the role of the unconscious mind in the quest of the hero. I had to later reconcile this early understanding of folk and fairy tales with what I learned about the Brothers Grimm: the fact that they were two rather stodgy, middle-class scholars who copied down stories told to them by relatives and nannies and who did not wander around the German countryside collecting stories from peasants. It was a blow to my understanding of story. I may have learned I was something of a romantic when it came to stories, but I also learned I didn't care. The Brothers Grimm altered, rewrote, Christianized, and recast their stories into a middle-class context. But isn't that the job of the storyteller? You take an old story, and you reshape it through the lens of your own experience.

Storytelling is about narrative, but it's also about engagement. The teller offers the tale, and the listener receives it. It's a fundamental and, in some important ways, primal mode of communication. The story is a distilled expression of experience, and the fairy tale is a form of expression that speaks to someone through his or her symbolic brain, by which I mean that part of the brain that understands dreams and dreaming.

Fractured fairy tales are another form of expression, but they are also about play. Taking familiar stories and altering details or endings relies on the listener's experience of story. If you don't know the story of "Goldilocks and the Three Bears," then you might think that "Goldilocks and the Three Pigs" is just silly. Such stories carry an implied understanding shared by teller and listener alike.

I encourage everyone to have fun with such stories. It's especially fun to tell a fractured fairy tale to a child. You can watch that child's eyes light up as they realize the story isn't quite what it's supposed to be. Children do this all the time. They make up stories and play at being their favorite characters; they use stories to have fun, to socialize, and to help sort out their problems, which are deeper and more complex than most adults can appreciate.

It wasn't until I began writing a blog that I tried my hand at writing fractured fairy tales, and to my surprise, I liked it. Most of the sixteen stories here first appeared on my blog. As I gathered them for this collection, I was also surprised to see that most of them were about female heroes. It makes sense, though. I had spent my life as a father raising daughters and trying to understand the world from a girl's perspective. Rereading these stories confirmed something else for me. When I'm thinking about stories, I'm thinking about my daughters—the trials they've encountered growing up, the ways they've had to make sense of the world, and those many, many evenings telling stories at bedtime.

WT, November, 2015

53379307R00125

Made in the USA
Charleston, SC
11 March 2016